WHAT READERS ARE S
THE TRUE LIES OF REMBRANDT STONE:

This book is so good. As soon as you have an idea of what might happen, the author throws you a curveball. The suspense and mystery of this plot is a twenty on a scale of one to ten. I highly recommend this book. – *Karen, Goodreads*

You know that beginning on the roller coaster feeling? That click, click, click climbing feeling? The anticipation that builds in your gut and your entire being braces for the rush? That is The True Lies of Rembrandt Stone. – *Kelly, Goodreads*

I'm not a fast reader, but when it comes to a Rembrandt Stone book, you can guarantee that I'll read it in one day. This story is just so captivating that there's really nothing that can be done other than read it the moment it hits my Kindle. – *Mimi, Goodreads*

I can't recommend this series enough. It has suspense, it has a complicated multi level mystery thread, it has characters that feel so real, it has an absolutely beautiful love story. It has everything. – *Nicole, Goodreads*

As a reader, there are few things more satisfying to me than a book that makes me completely abandon my own reality for the sake of the characters within the pages. This entire series is a master class in accomplishing just that. – *Courtney, Soul of a Librarian*

I basically devoured this book. Like all the other books in the series, once you start it's hard to stop, and then at the end you're dying to read the next book. – *Tressa, Wishful Endings*

I am LOVING this series! It's so hard to put these books down. They grab you from the first page and before you know it it's 2am and you still don't want to stop reading! – *Shirley*

The excitement, suspense and need to know what happens next builds with every release in this unique and astonishing series. Definitely start with book one and you'll be hooked by these novels that you can't put down. – *Kim H*

THE TRUE LIES
OF REMBRANDT STONE

BLOOD FROM A STONE

TRISTONE

TriStone Media Group
Minneapolis, MN

Tristone Media Inc.

15100 Mckenzie Blvd

Minnetonka, Minnesota, 55345

Copyright © 2021 by Tristone Media

ISBN: 978-1-954023-09-3

www.RembrandtStone.com

SOLI DEO GLORIA

CHAPTER 1

This is not my world.

Not my life.

Not my time.

Sure, it resembles a life I knew—from the snow piled up along the blackened, salted streets, the icy wind buffeting the frosty diner window, to the sound of Celine Dion singing how her heart will go on, and even the smell of oil in the fryers of the late-night diner. It could be any one of the diners I used to frequent in downtown Minneapolis after a long day of investigations.

But this is not my life.

My life is twenty years in the future, and right now, if fate were kind, or even fair, I would be reading *Llama, Llama, Red Pajama* to my seven-year-old blonde cherub as she clutches a ratty one-eyed bear named Gomer and tells me to slow down, to read it again.

My gorgeous wife, Eve, would be standing in the doorway of our partially remodeled craftsman located in a suburb of Uptown. Or maybe she'd be across the hall in our king bed, bundled up in her wool socks and thick bathrobe, her reading glasses down on her nose, deep in the latest issue of the *Journal for Forensic Scientists*.

Downstairs, the light in my den would be on, the cursor at my computer blinking, waiting for me to continue my half-finished novel.

And I would be happy. Until now, I wouldn't realize how happy, but as I sit here, I know.

I had a happy ending.

This is not it. But this time around, if I'm smart, I'll win.

I must win.

To a time traveler, until you've been someplace for a long time, rewriting the past feels like a game. We jump into the moment, armed with knowledge we shouldn't possess, the older and wiser versions of ourselves, with the goal of rewriting our lives, this time for the better.

For us, the game isn't win or lose, but rather, scored on the what-ifs that we grab, the shouldas we accomplish. And, all the while, in the back of our minds, if we make a wrong move, we're buoyed by the surety it can be reset.

It's taken me four rounds, but this time I know.

This is not a game.

Time is playing for keeps and there's no reset if I fail.

But don't worry—this time, I will not be bested.

I swear it on my life.

I keep that information tucked inside, my countenance cool, as I sit in a booth, across from a man long since dead, but now very much alive, Minneapolis Police Chief John Booker. My mentor, friend and the man who will save my life in roughly six minutes and forty-two seconds.

In Jin's Liquors, the store next door, right now, a robbery is going down, and if we don't leave now, the owner will be shot in the chest by a Colt .38. He'll bleed out in less than five minutes, but before collapsing, he'll pull his alarm.

And because Booker and I are next door, we'll respond.

I should probably mention that I'm a homicide investigator with the Minneapolis Police Department. When I left my world, last time around, I was also the interim police chief, so at this point I'm pretty good at this game.

I'll go in first, breaking through the front doors, and see the downed owner. Going immediately to his aid, I won't see the perp coming out of the back room hauling the contents of the safe. I also won't see him aim his gun at me and pull the trigger.

I especially won't see Booker push me away, behind a display of Seagram's wine coolers.

The gunshot will hit the chief.

He'll die beside the owner within the next two minutes, leaving a legacy of heroism, and taking with him a slew of questions I now need answers to.

But we'll get to those.

Because this time, he will live. I've studied every detail of this scene.

I know how to win.

"So, tell me, Rem, how's she doing?"

We're talking about my current partner, rookie investigator Shelby Ruthers. In *my* time, at least my most recent version, she's the Minneapolis police chief.

Here, I'm tasked with training her. And apparently, Booker is keenly interested in her progress.

At least, I think that's why we're sitting in a diner on a Friday night at 10 p.m. eating pie.

Maybe he has something else on his mind—I don't know. I've never lived this rewrite of time before.

The details of his death I learned from his jacket, the one included in my stack of cold case files, his killer never apprehended.

9

But that file is never going to be made.

Like I said, things will go down differently this time.

This time, I'll get there early. And maybe I won't be able to save the life of the owner, but John Booker will not die.

Neither will I.

The perp will get away, at least for the next forty-eight hours. I know what you're thinking, but he *will* go down for his crimes. Just not yet.

Before then I have to bring another murderer to justice.

The man who killed my wife.

It's a long story, so wait for it. Because, right now, I just need to answer Booker, then figure out how to get next door before the alarm sounds.

Before history repeats itself.

"She's nailing it," I say to his question about Shelby and take a sip of coffee. I like this place—it's a tucked away diner in a strip mall near Chicago Avenue and 36th just outside of Downtown Minneapolis. They serve killer pies, and sometimes Booker and I sneak away for the house special—Grandma Lou's Lemon Angel chiffon.

The place is unimpressive—a long counter display that shows the various pies, a few drugstore stools mounted in front of the Formica counter, retro tables with vinyl yellow chairs and cafe curtains at the window.

But the pie—oh, I'd forgotten how the lemon tart dissolves in your mouth with just the right balance of salty, lard-based crust, and a hint of fluffy meringue. It's almost enough to distract me.

Not quite. I have an eye on the parking lot, looking for movement. Last time, the perp escaped out the back, and I've already spotted a door to the back of the diner.

But, like I said, I don't want to catch the shooter. Not yet. He's not why I'm here. Just a by-product, collateral justice, as it were. But the moment he's caught is the moment this ride through time ends.

And I've got stuff to do, places to be before I close the books on this jump.

"That's good," Booker says, still talking about Shelby, "because Danny hired her on your recommendation. But we need to get her trained because Burke is finished with his assignment with Danny's task force, now that Hassan Abdilhali is dead. His gang is in disarray, and the Minneapolis drug trade is ripe for a new regime."

"So, Burke is looking for a new partner?" I take another bite of pie—my last one, because I've gotta figure out how to leave in about forty seconds.

Booker gives me a wry grin. He's always seemed a man from a different time, as if he walked straight from the pages of *Lonesome Dove*, fresh from leading a posse, a wizened look of battle in his eyes. He is tall, with slightly graying hair, and speaks with a low baritone, his words slow, thoughtful. But his dark brown eyes are always studying, weighing.

I wonder if I measure up.

"Burke will always be your partner, Rem. You know that." Booker takes a sip of his coffee.

It's then I notice he's wearing a wedding ring, and my mind flips back to the woman I met back in my real time, a reporter named Frankie.

The daughter Booker never had in our original timeline.

So, he's married, although if my memory of Frankie's story is correct, he and her mother are separated.

Frankie will lose her father tonight if my rewrite doesn't take.

I glance out the window, toward the street and frown. A ruse, but Booker notices. "What?"

"Thought I saw something…" I get up, move toward the door, and he follows.

"What did you see?"

"Isn't the liquor store closed?" I push out into the night, knowing he'll follow.

Around the force, I'm known for my hunches. You know by now what they are—foreknowledge. And maybe Booker knows it too. But he's on my tail because I'm also a cop and I see things that shouldn't be.

It's late January, and my breath fogs the air, the chill finding my nose, slithering down my neck. The fresh snowfall is piled up around the perimeter of the lot, and an icy layer of danger coats the steps and sidewalks.

Streetlights shine against the dark windows of the liquor store, but as we walk down the sidewalk, a light flashes in the back.

Cheater, you say, but gimmie a break, I need an edge if I hope to pull this off.

We pause outside the window, and it's then the gunshot barks.

No alarm, not yet, and I hoof it down to the door. It's locked, the closed sign on it, but a glance inside shows the owner down, writhing and bleeding out.

He might live if we can get to him. In my previous go-round, according to the file, I kicked the door in.

This time I say, "Call it in!" Then take off for the back of the building.

The back door is open, and if I stage this right, no one will die.

I figure, if Booker can't get inside, he can't get shot, right?

I spot a car idling in the back. It's a Toyota Supra, a hotrod wanna be, but it has nothing on my Porsche, bless her, now a sooty shell back in my time. I snapshot the license plate in my mind and move toward the door.

It's unlocked.

My plan is simple. Slip inside, making enough noise that the perp hears me and flees. And I'll let him go, for now. I'll pull the owner behind the counter—maybe save his life—and only after the perp has escaped will I unlock the front door.

And Booker will live.

One game point for Rembrandt Stone.

I steal in and spot a light on in the back office, a lamp. The alarm is still sounding, so it might mask my noise, but even so, I hustle to the front of the building, grabbing a towel off a mop and rack sitting near the door.

The owner is groaning, laying near the front checkout desk and I kneel before him. He's a middle-aged Korean man, and the shot has hit him in his upper right side. "Hang in there," I say as I shove the towel against his wound.

He grabs my wrist, and it's stronger than I would imagine. "Help."

The words still me because he's a ghost from the grave.

"Jin-Sun...my...daughter..."

My eyes widen because I don't remember a daughter in the report.

"Where?"

"In...office...

I bite back a word, then swallow and nod.

And that's when I hear the voice that chills me through. "Rem. We have backup coming."

Booker has come in the front. I don't know if he's broken the lock, or simply slammed through the glass, but he now stands between me and the perp, who, by my estimation, is still emptying the safe.

With Jin-Sun hiding nearby.

And now the game has changed.

Booker is the target. And time is trying to win.

I can almost hear the laughter.

I figure one of two things could happen.

Booker will still get shot. And Frankie will grow up without her father. And the recent past will spool out like it did before—with Danny Mulligan becoming police chief, and his daughter, Eve, who I love, moving to Florida, out of his protective reach.

I will lose her all over again to a Miami cop named Val.

And Val will lead us to a serial killer who takes Eve's life.

And sure, there are thousands of ways that might change, but with each variation, each rewrite, my life veers even further off course. Brings me back to another world that has been rewritten into another unlivable version of the life I should have.

No. Not this time.

This time, everything will be different.

Of course, there is option two, where Booker will hear—and catch the perp—before he gets off his lethal shot. Maybe even kill him.

Which means this cold case is solved.

I will then immediately return to the dismal future I left, with me sitting in the rain outside the graveyard where my daughter and my wife are buried.

If that happens, I won't have time to track down Leo Fitzgerald, the serial killer who, in my time, has murdered thirty-eight women, including my daughter. I won't have time to propose to Eve, and keep her from moving to Florida. I won't even have time to chop down the massive elm tree that will someday take out the craftsman home Eve and I love.

I know this is not about a tree, but as long as I'm counting my losses…

Thankfully, fate and I have been in the ring together before. It tried to steal my wife from me, three different ways.

Stole my partner from me.

Killed Booker in every timeline so far.

And swept my daughter and her memory from the face of the earth.

But what fate has forgotten is that I don't know what's good for me. And I'll keep swinging no matter how many times I get knocked flat.

I possess all the cheats.

And, I have nothing left to lose.

"Get down!" I get up, draw my weapon and point to the back—the wall, really, and pull off a shot. Booker turns, as if following my actions and that's when I dive at him.

It happens fast, so fast that Booker can't have noticed that indeed, no one stands in the back to take him out.

Yet.

We land in a painful tangle behind the display of Seagram's wine coolers, which crash around us in a splatter of glass and sticky, sweet alcohol.

A shot fires behind me. The front glass door shatters.

I scramble off Booker and glance in the back.

The perp bursts through the door, into the night.

Yes!

I'm instantly on my feet and running hard to the door in false pursuit.

The getaway car has taken off, the taillights fading as it rounds the end of the strip mall, into the night.

Muffled sobbing, a hiccup of sound emerges from the office and I fear what I'll find.

The desk lamp splashes wan light into the room. A floor safe is open, the contents—mostly paper—spilled onto the floor.

The sounds come from under the desk. I walk over, then crouch and finally hit my hands and knees. "Jin-Sun?"

She's young—maybe nine years old, with big brown eyes and dark hair. She's sitting with her knees pulled to her chest, making herself small.

"You're safe." I keep my voice soft, gentle, a remnant of time when I was a father to a seven-year-old daughter. My throat thickens at the flash of memory, my Ashley sitting on her bed, her blue eyes thick with tears as she implores me to find Gomer, a silly bear I gave her for her fourth birthday. *But Daddy, you're a detective. You know how to find things..*

I do, honey. And I'm going to find you, I promise.

I hold out my hand to Jin-Sun. "Come out. No one will hurt you."

She stares at my offering, and then places her hand in mine. It's soft, but she hangs on and I pull her out of the darkness. She stands before me, and then throws her arms around me.

My breath rushes out of me and I can't help but wrap an arm around her, bracing myself with the other hand on the desk. "Everything is going to be okay," I whisper, and the words sink into me.

It's the last thing I said to Eve, right before Leo Fitzgerald kidnapped her and killed her.

I close my eyes, but the memory burns through me.

Eve, lying in my family's barn, her body gray and lifeless, a twenty-dollar bill—the calling card of the Jackson killer—in her grip.

Forcing the image away, I stand up and take Jin-Sun's hand. Sirens scream through the air, and as we walk out of the office, I see

Booker letting EMTs inside.

Jin-Sun squeezes my hand as they run up to her father, un-moving on the floor. I crouch next to her. "Honey, don't be afraid. They're going to help your daddy."

She looks at me though, with those big brown eyes and nods. "I'm not afraid."

"You're not?"

She shakes her head. "I prayed while I was hiding, and God sent you."

I have nothing.

I don't know why, but I can't help but feel that fate has won, again.

And I wonder who, really, is doing the cheating.

CHAPTER 2

The sky at midnight is the same, whatever timeline I'm in. A dark arc over the city, stars that seem to blink down at me, seeing me.

I can't escape the knowledge that wherever I go, fate knows my name.

I'm standing on the sidewalk, my breath turning to tufts of smoke in the frigid night air, and I'm freezing, having just retrieved my jacket from Jin-Sun, who has been rescued by her mother.

Apparently, she's separated from Min-Jin, the father, and he took his child to work today.

I'm sure that won't play well in divorce court.

At least, however, Min-Jin is still alive and on his way to Hennepin County Medical Center.

An Integra pulls in, and the funny coil in my chest eases.

I know it's been thirty years on the job together, but somehow, when my partner Andrew Burke shows up, time clicks into place.

I belong with Burke, like Riggs belongs with Danny.

He's not on duty yet, but because it's me, he's shown up. When he gets out of the car, I see he's wearing a long gray wool coat, and is dressed in a suit.

Right, he's fresh off a gig. In his off time, Burke is a jazz drummer for a local band. And, sliding out of the passenger side is Shelby. She's wearing a little black dress, boots and a long black coat.

I can't help but smile because my guess is that they're dating.

I set that up. In our original timeline, Burke was single. Along the way, he married my Eve, but I fixed that. In our last iteration, he and Shelby were married and have a beautiful baby daughter, Daphne.

At least I've made one good move. Fingers crossed it stays that way.

"Rem," Burke says as he reaches me. "What happened?" Concern edges his voice, and maybe it's because my shirt is bloodied although I've washed my hands.

"I'm not hurt," I say, just to reassure him, but his concern is not without merit. Over the past three jumps into the past, I've been stabbed, beaten, and nearly burned to death.

Not to mention I've totaled my car, nearly been shot and most recently, drowned, although that was in a future I hope to delete.

Maybe I should be a little more worried, come to think of it.

An officer on the scene has already taken my statement, but I'll sum up for Burke and Shelby.

I skip over the pie and go right to, "I saw a flicker of light from the darkened shop, and it brought me out to the street."

The key to lying is to believe your own words, so I've conjured up the flash of light, the flicker of it off the snow of the parking lot. It's a trick I perfected while undercover for nearly a decade, and now the lie slides out of me without a glitch.

"We heard a shot and I went around to the back and came in through the open door. I must have missed seeing the perp in the office—I was just trying to get to the victim."

Burke stands with his hands in his pockets, and Shelby looks past me, into the store, as if drawing a mental picture. She's pretty—her blonde hair flowing out of a dark stocking hat. Burke, too, is wearing a baseball cap over his short dark hair.

You won't have that hair much longer, buddy, I want to say. Just go ahead and shave it. Instead, "I saw the perp come out of the office—we must have startled him—and took a shot. Then I dove at Booker."

"Saved my life," Booker says as he walks up to us. His face is grim, but he nods, and then clamps his hand on my shoulder. "I didn't even see him."

Because the perp wasn't there, but no one is the wiser.

"Did you get a glimpse of him?" Shelby asks.

"No, but I got the license plate."

"Me too," Booker says. He rattles it off. "Shelby, see if you can get a match. Car is a 1990 Toyota Supra."

Great. I'd hoped he'd missed that. Because Booker on his game might solve this case before breakfast.

And I have things to do first.

"There were two of them," I add. "A getaway driver."

"You're lucky he didn't hear you coming in," Burke says. "He could have surprised you before you saw him."

Luck is one way to describe it.

"Did anyone call CSI?" Shelby asks.

My thoughts go to Eve. As one of the Minneapolis PD crime scene investigators, she might be here.

I suddenly ache to see her. To hear her voice, touch her, know she's alive.

Still alive.

"Silas is on call, and he's on his way," Booker says.

Which means Eve is at home, her little bungalow on Webster

21

Street. And yeah, she's probably asleep, but she's getting used to me showing on up her doorstep at crazy hours, a little desperate.

It's one of my hallmark moves.

And the need to see her is suddenly, ferociously burning a hole through me.

"I gotta go," I say, and head out to my Jeep.

"Rem!" Booker's voice follows me, and I turn. The tall parking lot light splashes gold around me. The chief strides up to me, something enigmatic in his expression.

I'm expecting another thank you. Instead, "How did you know?"

I blink at him. "How did I—"

"You're back, aren't you?" He says it just above a whisper but it feels like he's shouting.

"Back?" It's almost a squeak, like I've forgotten all my training.

He cocks his head. "The other Rem. The old guy."

He's nailed me. I sigh. Then nod because it doesn't hurt to have an ally.

"I knew it." He puts his hands in his pockets, a grim set to his mouth and looks away, shaking his head. "You just can't get it through your head that you're not here to stop the crimes. You're here to—"

"Solve the case. I know. But this time, it was different. It was personal." And I give him a hard look.

Booker meets my gaze. It takes a moment, but, "It was me this time, wasn't it?"

I plead the fifth.

"You didn't see the shooter before you tackled me, did you? That was all an act."

I look away. "Frankie deserves her father," I say quietly. And then I meet his gaze. "And your wife deserves a second chance."

His eyes widen. "What—"

"That's all you get. Just…don't give up quite so easily." I turn up my collar, zip my coat all the way up to keep in what little warmth is forming. "You don't know when it could all be ripped away."

He stares at me, frowning, maybe a little rattled. "Rem, what happened?"

I close my eyes, and the urge to tell him rushes over me, nearly buckles my knees. *God, I need a friend, someone—*

His hand slides onto my shoulder and I open my eyes. "I get it. Knowing you could stop the suffering is…well, it gets into your bones."

I open my mouth because I can see it in his eyes.

He went back and changed something. I already know this, because I remember the old version of my life, the original version. My brother, Mickey, kidnapped at age nine. His body found fifteen years later in Gray's Lake, near my childhood home. The killer still free.

The current version, the one everybody else knows, the one I can't remember, is that Booker caught the murderer and found my brother's body before it could sink into the mud.

"I know you changed the past," I say, my voice cutting low. "I know you caught Mickey's murderer."

He blinks at me, frowns, "How—?"

"I don't know. I remember the first version—the one where—"

"He's found just a few months ago," Booker finishes.

I nod.

He sighs, looks away, shakes his head, then turns back to me. "I should have caught him the first time. I was on his trail—I was investigating a string of murders in the city. Boys your brother's age who went missing. All of them were lured by a man driving an ice cream truck. A white van."

A white van.

I draw in a breath.

I saw a white van pass me on the road the day we were out riding our bikes, moments before Mickey went missing.

"How did you catch him?"

He sighed. "I cheated, of course. I went back to your brother's case, knowing where he'd bury him, and waited for him to…"

"To dump my brother's body."

He nods, but can't look at me. And I know why. "Why couldn't you have gone to a different case? Found one of their bodies? Stopped the crime before it happened?" Saved Mickey.

His eyes close, as if in pain. "Mickey was my only lead—his was the only body that was ever found."

"But you could have gone to the scene of a previous crime—"

Booker shoots me an exasperated look.

"Because I was afraid of what might happen if I changed things, again!"

I frown at him, step back.

Booker glares at me, shakes his head. "Rem, you do know that every time you change something, fate fights back. It adjusts. And in the end—"

"Fate wins." My mouth tightens.

He nods. "You can't fix it all. Something will break. And I was…I was afraid of what else might break."

I stare at him. "What did you break, Booker?"

Something I can't place flashes across his face. He shakes his head. "I'm sorry, Rem. I'm so sorry for all of it."

"Sorry for *what*?"

"Just be careful." He meets my eyes. "You don't know whose lives you'll destroy—"

"How about my own?" The chill is gone, and a coal flares in my gut. "How about *my* life? Does fate care at all about the lives I save, the crimes I solve—the people I love?" I take a step toward him, and cut my voice low, although, honestly, I don't care what anyone thinks.

I'm probably already losing myself, fractured into so many timelines, I don't know what is true.

Except, yes, I do.

I have a constant, a through line. Something to center me and keep me fast to the journey.

My love for Eve. My love for Ashley. And now, the sense that this is my last shot to get it right.

Like I said, I have nothing to lose, so I look at Booker and say, calmly, "Eve is dead."

He frowns. "What—? Now?"

"No. In my time."

I check for other ears near us because now it's going to get weird. Silas has arrived with the CSI van, and Burke is talking with him as crime scene techs tape off the scene.

Shelby is trailing a photographer, pointing out shots. No wonder she became chief.

I turn back to Booker and cut my voice low. "I came back last summer to catch the coffee shop bomber, and when I got back to present day, my daughter, my seven-year-old daughter, had been *murdered.*"

Booker draws in a breath, his mouth tight.

"Then I came back to save Danny Mulligan's life and when I returned, my wife was married to my best friend! And Ashley—had never existed at all."

Booker swallows.

"And then, I saved Burke and two children from a fire, and

25

that time when I got back, yes, I had Eve…but fate chased me back to the present and now *she's dead*. My wife, my Eve, is murdered in my time."

"Wow, Rem," Booker says, and it looks like he's going to do something stupid like touch my arm but I pull away.

"I'm going to kill him," I say. My breath is leaking out, trembling.

"Rembrandt—"

"I *won't* lose her again!" I back away from him, hold my hand up, willing my voice back to myself. "Not again."

Eve is mine, and death cannot have her. "This time, I win. And after I get my life back, I'm taking this watch and drowning it in the middle of Lake Minnetonka."

His jaw tightens.

"See, I agree with you. No one should have the power to change time."

I leave him in the cold, barren parking lot.

I have only one destination on my mind.

Eve's house is dark as I pull up. Of course it is—it's after midnight, and even the street light in front of her place has kicked off. The front drive is shoveled—I hope I've had a hand in that—and her porch salted. She lives in a small one and a half story bungalow in the heart of the Uptown area, most of it remodeled.

Eve is smart, creative, beautiful and right now, *alive*.

You have to know I barely stop myself from simply walking into her house, running upstairs, bursting into her bedroom and taking her into my arms.

I probably hang on her doorbell a little too long. I brace myself on the frame as listen for her footsteps. Close my eyes as they sound on the stairs.

The Eve of now is not the Eve of my future, I know this. My

Eve has lived with me, knows my impulses, my dark places, my regrets.

My Eve looks at the man I am, knows where I've come from, and loves me anyway.

My Eve is also the director of the Minneapolis Crime Lab. She's smart, published, celebrated and respected.

This Eve is young, brave, eager and wants to impress.

And she's impressed by me, Rembrandt the younger, who is published, drives a Corvette and is one of the youngest investigators in the Minneapolis Police Department.

I need to remember *this* Rembrandt before she opens the door and finds the older, grieving and desperate me. The me who can still feel her lifeless body in my arms.

Eve opens the door, and I take a breath. Because old me is winning as she stands there, dressed in her long pajama pants, thick wool socks, and a fluffy purple bathrobe. Her red hair is wild around her head and I need to run my fingers through it, feel the softness…

She blinks at me. "Rembrandt?" She glances past me, into the night, and then back at me. "Are you okay?"

I am not.

All I can do is give a weak nod.

"Come inside." She opens the door and steps back.

Of course I come in. Because she smells of the shampoo she used, and looks so pretty and sweet and frankly, she's a bastion of shelter in this game of war.

And I need a moment. Just one moment of peace to catch my breath.

To gather my wits.

To remind myself that I can win.

She closes the door behind me. "Rem, are you hurt?"

I turn to her, swallow. And my hand lifts to her face, touching it.

She is real.

My throat tightens.

Then, all of it rushes over me and I pull her to myself, hard, my arms around her. "Eve," I say, and bury my face into her neck.

Her arms are around me, too, and she lets me hold on.

Eve is life.

I don't know how long I stand there. Not long enough, forever wouldn't be long enough, but I finally let her go. She steps back, and puts her warm hands on my cold, chapped face. "You're scaring me."

I take her hands. "Everything is fine," I lie. And then I know why I'm here.

My gaze scans her face, and it's all right there—our future, the years we'll have. The fights, the forgiveness…Ashley.

I kiss her. It's not gentle, nor is it desperate, just the kiss that tells her what I already know.

I am hers.

And she is mine.

I back her up to the wall, and brace one arm over her shoulder, slowing down my touch. She puts her hands on my chest, and it's not to keep me away, but to pull me closer.

I'm starting to like these late-night visits, probably too much.

I kiss her slowly, drinking her in, reminding myself that I am not supposed to know her as well as I do. But the room is warming and she molds herself against me and if we don't stop soon, I'll be lost.

I very much want to be lost. And probably, never found.

Instead, I remember the man that I want to be and pull myself away. I brace my other hand over her shoulder, meet her eyes.

"Marry me, Eve."

Her's widen as she draws in a breath. "What?"

"Marry me."

A swallow. "I don't—Rem—"

"Listen, I know we've only been dating a few months, but…I love you, Eve. And I always will. But…*please*." I refuse to let desperation leak into my voice, but you know it's there.

She puts her hand on my chest. "Rem, listen. I know that… that something happened, but it's…"

"Fast. I know." I take her hands. "I know I'm impulsive. And this sounds a little crazy but," I step closer to her. "I don't want to wait. I don't want anything to happen—"

She steps away. "What do you mean, happen?"

And I haven't said it right, I know that, but I want her inside my head, seeing our future like I do, so I put my forehead to hers. "Someday, Eve, we'll have a beautiful craftsman home that you'll constantly want to remodel, and a swing set in the backyard, a deck with a barbecue and a beautiful daughter with blonde hair and a pink bedroom and a thousand stuffed animals and we'll take her to the beach and to the park, and I'll write a novel—"

She leans away at that. "You won't be a detective?"

"I will. But I'll also write in this magic leather chair you'll give me—"

"And what will I do?" She's smiling now, and I might be winning.

"You'll be the head of your department, an award-winning, published forensic scientist and still the most beautiful woman I know."

Her eyes are glistening. "You see all that for us?"

All that, and more. "Yes."

I expect her to kiss me. To say yes. To put her arms around me.

To make my world whole.

Instead, she looks down from me. Closes her eyes, as if in pain.

Oh no. "What?"

She turns back to me, a storm in her eyes. "I can't, Rem."

I blink at her. "You *can't?*"

"Part of me wants to say yes…" She ducks out from under my arms, turns, her hands clutching her sides. "It's just…" She takes what seems to be a fortifying breath, and in it I find my own held. "But I still have other things I want to do with my life."

Florida.

The idea sits in my brain like an ember. And maybe that's not at all on her radar, but it's right about now in our pre-rewritten past that she'll get the offer for Florida, start considering it.

"Whatever you want, I want," I say to her. My voice is soft, almost pleading. "I just want us to do it together."

This has her attention. "I do too." She takes a step closer, her hand on my chest. "Why do you always seem to read my mind? To know my thoughts?"

Of course I'm cheating, but I lower my voice, and my words are truthful. "Because I know you, Eve."

She draws in a breath, and her gaze roams my face.

"I should go," I say, suddenly aware that the room has warmed, my heartbeat is loud and I'm dreaming of the Eve she will be.

"Stay." She moves back into my arms, and it's not hard to agree since the last thing, the *very* last thing I want to do is walk back out into that cold.

She kisses my neck, and my entire body says yes. *Stay.*

In the back of my mind, I know I could stay.

I *very much* could stay, and then maybe she gets pregnant, and…

We start the cycle again.

But I have pledged to be a better man this time around. If only to earn points with fate.

Because I must bring Eve back.

Breathe, Rem. "How about we have dinner. Tonight. Talk about it?" I sound like my normal, reasonable self. I ease her away from me with all the strength I possess.

But inside, you know, I'm hitting the bag down at the gym and shouting at the top of my lungs.

She nods, and the shouting stops, at least for the moment.

I kiss her forehead now. Meet her beautiful hazel-green eyes. "Everything is going to be all right, I promise."

Her eyes glisten and she nods.

She hasn't said yes. But she will.

And she will be safe. Because Leo Fitzgerald is next on my list of to-dos.

I step out into the frigid night, the spectators overhead silent.

And I wonder who they are rooting for.

CHAPTER 3

Let me be clear here. In all my twenty years as an inspector for the Minneapolis Police Department, and before that, as a beat cop, I never, not once, killed anyone.

I drew my service weapon plenty of times, used it on a few dire occasions, but no one ever died.

I'm not a killer. At least up till now, I haven't been.

Leo Fitzgerald changed all that. By proxy, somehow, my choices have killed thirty-eight women.

Even so, this is different.

This is premeditated.

A fist sits in my gut, squeezing tighter with every inch of the rising sun.

You can see why I couldn't sleep. Why I rose, showered, cleaned my Glock, then drove out to the home of Helen Fitzgerald, where Leo still lives in a small rambler located just outside the tiny town of Montrose.

A white Ford Fiesta that's seen a rough winter, given the rust over the wheel wells, sits in the driveway, and the walk is cleared to the house. A half melted snowman sits on the front porch, and the

Christmas lights still hang from the gutters.

For the last hour, I've been sitting on the street in my Jeep in the predawn, contemplating my decision.

The Jackson killer murdered thirty-eight women. Hunted them. Ran them down. Sexually assaulted them. Strangled them.

He set a trap for John Booker and ambushed him at this very house, setting off a bomb.

He kidnapped and murdered my daughter.

And most recently, he kidnapped and murdered my wife.

I'm starting to reframe this whole story because it feels like justice, doesn't it?

My Glock sits on the passenger seat, the sunrise glinting off the black metal.

But, it's still murder.

I lean my head back against the headrest and close my eyes.

Sometimes—most of the time—I wish the watch had never come to me.

A knock at the window opens my eyes. I sit up.

Staring at me through the window is a much younger version of the woman I met in a nursing home in Florida a few days and twenty-three years into the future.

Helen Fitzgerald.

She wears an oversized parka, a pair of sloppy boots and holds her morning paper in one hand, her bobbed blonde hair blowing into her face. In her mid-fifties, she has a kind face, and if I remember correctly, she's an elementary teacher. "Can I help you?"

I hope she hasn't seen the weapon on my seat. I lean up to block her view and roll down my window. "Hello. I'm…a friend of Leo's." The lie feels a little harder to this fourth-grade teacher. "I've come a long way," (true, if you count time) "and I was hoping to see him."

"Lenny's not home yet, but you look cold. Would you like a cup of coffee?"

A cup of coffee while I wait for her son to arrive so I can kill him? It's the stuff of a Lifetime movie, but I find myself nodding.

She walks away and I lock my Glock in the glove compartment.

Because the fist is still in my gut.

I'm certainly not going to kill a man in front of his *mother*.

The house is tidy, albeit small. A front room with hardwood floors, a couple overstuffed sofas, an eat-in kitchen with dark-paneled cupboards, yellow Formica counters. The aroma of coffee greets me and lures me in as I take my shoes off at the door and follow her in my stocking feet to the kitchen table.

"Are you a friend from the military?"

"Sort of," I say. "We've been through a lot together."

She pours me a mug of coffee. "Cream or sugar?"

"Black."

She puts the cup on the table. Pours herself a cup. "I don't know when Lenny will be home. Let me check his schedule."

I take a sip as I wait. It's acrid, thick and bracing.

The perfect pre-murder drink, maybe. I set the coffee down. "What's he doing these days?"

"Oh, he's a long haul driver. Gone for days at a time." Helen pulls a list of times off a Post-It note on the fridge. "Looks like he's due back tomorrow morning."

I knew he was a trucker, but I hadn't realized he'd been at that gig for so long. I wonder if he's left bodies in other states.

"Did you serve with him in the Big Red One?"

His military outfit, the First Army Division. He has a BRO tattoo on his arm from his days in Desert Storm.

"No. We met later. But I was in town and I thought I'd look

him up." My gaze goes to a grouping of pictures hanging on the living room wall. I get up. "Is this Lenny?" I point to his senior picture. He's wearing a purple and white letter jacket, a football emblem on the sleeve. "He played football?"

She has risen. "Oh yes. Was a defensive back. Their team won the state championship his junior year." She points to another picture, this time of the team, a lineup of handsome young teenagers.

My mind goes to Leo's ring. A *state championship* ring.

And for some reason, her words, some twenty years from now, find me. *Stop, Johnny, don't hurt him!*

Time will not be generous to Helen. She'll start showing signs of Alzheimer's in less than ten years, and by the time we meet, her mind will be caught in snapshots of the past, broken into pieces of recognition and confusion.

She will mistake me for a man I don't know named Johnny.

You did this! You—you made Lenny cry! He trusted you, and you made him cry!

Those words, shouted at me as I exited her room echo now, and I turn to her. "Helen, did Lenny have a friend named Johnny?"

I don't know why I'm asking. Maybe because of Lenny's future muttered words about Eve, right before he died. *"Johnny took her."*

Until this moment, I thought Johnny was a memory, a ghost from his days in Iraq, still alive in Leo's head.

Maybe he still is.

"Oh yes," she says. "The other defensive back—Gio—Johnny—Rossi." She points to his picture. He's blond and wide-shouldered, his hair long, and he's grinning.

"They look alike."

She nods. "Yes, they do." She turns away to the kitchen and offers nothing more, but there's something in her tone that lodges curiosity inside me.

"Lenny told me about a girl named Julia." No, Lenny told me that Johnny *killed* Julia, but maybe she's not dead yet.

She's stopped at the counter, put her coffee down and her shoulders rise and fall at my question.

Then she nods and turns. "Julia Pike. She was his first girlfriend." She walks over and puts her coffee cup into the sink. "She was the victim of a hit and run."

I follow her into the kitchen, not sure how to pose my next question. "Lenny once told me that Johnny might have had something to do with it."

To my surprise, Helen turns and her eyes are wet. "I don't know, but...there was always something about Johnny that unnerved me. He was...protective of Lenny. Overprotective."

"You think Johnny was trying to protect Lenny? From Julia?"

"She was such a sweet girl." She wipes her cheek. "But she was too young for him. Fifteen. And when her father found out, he put the kibosh on their relationship. Lenny was devastated."

I still because I'm seeing a pattern she probably doesn't want to know about.

Lenny dated Lauren Delaney and killed her when she broke it off with him.

And, he also killed Gretchen Anderson, a woman he dated.

She looks away from me, at the pictures on the wall. "It's my fault, of course."

I finish my coffee and hand her the cup. "Why?"

Her mouth tightens, as if she's considering her words. It's too late, but I probably should have mentioned I'm a detective.

But that was back when I wanted to kill Leo where he stood. Now, I can admit, that desire—or rather, purpose—is waning.

Eve has already connected his DNA to Lauren Delany's death. And, by now he's murdered Gretchen.

I could arrest him, and if justice wins, he'll be locked up and not a threat to Eve.

If justice wins.

"Because Lenny and Johnny are half brothers."

I know—her words hit me the same way. Half *brothers?* What?

She looks at me, and my face apparently says, *'splain, please,* because she sighs and says, "I dated Alfonzo Rossi while he and his wife were separated. Except, they weren't. He lied to me, and when I found out she was pregnant, well, so was I."

I manage not to react, just nod. But that sounds like the makings of trouble, doesn't it? And, "It's a small town," I say quietly, summing up the story.

"Yes. I had a good job, and I didn't want to leave it. And then Judy discovered Alfonzo had a number of women around town and divorced him. He was killed in a car accident not long after, and Judy and I actually became friends. As did the boys. Johnny was about six months older than Lenny, and he became a sort of big brother."

She puts my mug into the sink, her back to me. "You just never know how your sins will turn out."

She has no idea how much I agree with her.

"You think Johnny killed Julia because she hurt Lenny," I say.

She doesn't look at me when she nods. Then, "I don't know." She turns back to me, and folds her arms around herself. "Johnny and Lenny were close. Very close. They enlisted together, and while they were overseas, Judy died. Which was probably a good thing, too, because Johnny was killed in action. Lenny came home...altered. Disturbed."

PTSD. Only they didn't recognize it as well back then.

"He's a good boy, my Lenny." She meets my eyes and takes a breath. "Is that what you wanted to know, Detective?"

My heart skips, but I stare at her, I'm pretty sure, non-plussed. She folds her arms. "Lenny told me about you. That you accused him of killing Lauren. That you beat him up—"

"That's not quite how it happened. For the record, he came at me, first."

She gives me a look, like she might slap me. I step back.

"I just need to talk to him."

Her mouth pinches, and maybe she can see through my lie. *Mostly* a lie. "If I leave my number, will you call me when he gets home?"

I reach for a Post-It pad I see on her counter. I write my cell number down, looking back up at her. "If he's innocent, then I just need some information to verify his alibi." I peel off the Post-It and hold out the yellow piece of paper.

She sighs and looks at the Post-It as if it's diseased. Then, finally she takes it from me. Puts it on the fridge. Turns back to me. "You need to stop looking at my son for answers and find the person who really did these terrible things."

I nod, like I might do just that.

As I walk toward the door, my gaze scans the pictures again. Leo, as a chubby faced, towheaded toddler. Leo, toothless, seven years old. Leo, as a middle schooler (no one looks good in seventh grade).

Leo, in his military uniform.

And Leo, in a group shot with what looks like members of his platoon. Guys in the desert camo of the army, holding M4 Carbines, some of them in grease paint, all grinning. A man has his arm over Leo's shoulders and I pause, study his face.

"That's Johnny," she says. "About six months before he died."

I look at her. "How did he die?"

"IED. Hit their entire caravan. Leo was injured, too. A severe concussion. Bad enough to bring him home."

That could account for his continuing trauma, the voices he still hears.

"Thank you for the coffee, Mrs. Fitzgerald."

"Latsky," she says. "I married about ten years ago. I'm a widow."

I look at her, the name lodging inside me. "What was your husband's name?"

"Nick. Nick Latsky. I know I should probably revert to my maiden name, but I'm not ready to let him go yet."

She picks up a wedding picture of a dark-haired man wearing a suit, late forties, holding Helen's hand.

"I'm sorry for your loss."

"Thank you, Detective." And she smiles, her kind eyes back.

I feel a little like I'm in fourth grade, having turned in my spelling words.

"My son is a good man. The war was hard on him, but he wouldn't hurt anyone."

When I get back into my Jeep, the coil is back in my gut.

No, I am not a murderer.

And for the first time, I'm not quite so sure Leo is either.

CHAPTER 4

No amount of sugar would solve Eve's problems.

"Some*body* couldn't sleep." The voice came from behind her as she studied the board of photos from last night's shooting in a liquor store off Chicago Avenue.

A shooting Rembrandt Stone had responded to before the alarm had even been pulled. A crime that, had he not seen the shooter, might have resulted in Chief Booker being killed.

Maybe that's what had Rembrandt so rattled last night when he'd arrived on her doorstep.

And...*proposed.*

"Seriously? A half box of donuts?"

She turned at Silas's question. He was holding up the box of Dunkin' Donuts, the half-empty remains of her early morning binge. Two glazed raised and a cake donut over the course of three hours didn't feel like a travesty, especially since she'd washed them down with black coffee as penance.

Rembrandt had her hooked on white chocolate mochas with a shot of raspberry and shoot, there he went again, tiptoeing into her brain, taking up too much space.

She'd left her house at 5 a.m. after giving up any attempt at sleep. Rembrandt kept showing up in her head, moving her into the wall, bracing his hand over her and leaning in for the kind of kiss that had her…had her offering to let him stay.

Oh boy.

She still couldn't believe that invitation had sneaked out of her. But she never did think straight with Rembrandt Stone in her airspace. Sure, their romance had progressed over the past few months, but when he showed up to *propose*…

Yeah, it was probably a good thing that he suggested dinner, a conversation in the light of day, and left.

Now, she walked over and took the box, swiped another donut and set it down on the table. "Better act fast if you want one."

Silas raised an eyebrow, then shook his head. "Coffee only. The last thing I need is sugar on four hours of sleep."

"You headed up the CSI team on this case?" She gestured to the pictures of the crime scene in Jin's Liquors.

He poured a cup of coffee from the pot in the workroom, then came back over to look at the board. Outside, the icy wind swept through the downtown streets, rattling the windows in the ancient City Hall building. Her view of the downtown area—the puffy metro dome, the shiny IDS building—was shunted by the layers of frost that curlicued up the window panes.

Inside, the crime lab was just starting to come alive, with techs arriving at their work tables, equipped with microscopes, desktop computers, and various lab equipment at their disposal—a florescence spectrometer, a fingerprint development chamber, a blood chemistry analyzer, chemical imagery systems and their newest acquisition, a DNA Sequencer.

Along the wall were chemical storage cabinets, forensic workstations, and equipment specifically designed to handle liquids.

She could analyze and provide facts, but it was up to Rembrandt Stone and his like to put it all together. Still, it was simply uncanny, sometimes, how he just *knew* things.

Like the hunch that led him over to Jin's Liquors even before the alarm sounded. His instincts had saved the owner's life.

"Yes," Silas said, coming to stand beside her as he stared at the board. "I also pulled all the security tapes to see if we could get an ID on the shooter."

"Great. Let's get them to Alice, and see if she can slow them down, get a good shot."

"Chief Booker also managed to grab the plate number off the car. We'll run it and see if we get a hit."

"Any fingerprints from the safe?"

"None, but we did pick up some fibers, as well as residue."

"Good. Get those analyzed, too."

"Already on it."

Of course he was. Silas had been her study mate at the university. Her work on the coffee shop bombings last summer had given her the early promotion.

Her first case with Rembrandt Stone.

"Do you have a copy of Rem's statement?" she asked Silas.

Marry me, Eve. His breath on her skin, hot, the taste of him as he kissed her, leaving no question—

Listen, I know we've only been dating a few months, but...I love you, Eve. And I always will.

"Rem?" Silas asked, his brow raised. "Not Inspector Stone?"

She looked at him, blinking.

Stay.

"Um...what?"

"Eve." Silas stepped in front of her, blocking her view of the board. "Are you in a sugar coma?"

43

Probably. Yes. But, "No. I'm …" She shook her head. "Rembrandt showed up on my doorstep last night and…" She glanced around, to the various techs, and back to Silas. He had short blond hair, blue eyes, wore a pair of dress pants and an oxford under his lab coat. Handsome—probably, at one time she had liked him enough to date him. Maybe he'd wanted it, too, although he'd never asked.

He didn't like Rembrandt. She wasn't sure why.

Still, he was her closest friend. "He asked me to marry him."

Silas didn't move, his mouth closing, his breath drawing in. Then, "Really?"

"Yeah." Her gaze went to the board behind Silas. Back to him. "Maybe he was rattled by the shooting, I don't know. But he was pretty…um…adamant."

He raised an eyebrow. "What did you say?"

She turned away from the board, walked to the window. Sighed. "I told him that…well, I wasn't sure. I still had other things I wanted to do with my life."

Silas said nothing, and frankly, she had to tell someone, so, "I might be moving to Florida."

Silence. And she turned.

He was frowning. "What are you talking about?"

She turned and leaned on the window ledge. "Okay, so you remember when my mom was shot last summer?"

"Of course."

"She's got a cousin who lives in Miami, and she called us, checking on Mom. We started talking, and she's a dispatcher with the Miami-Dade County Police Department. She got me in touch with the director of Forensics, and suddenly I was interviewing and being offered the job—"

"You got a job offer in Florida? Why didn't you tell me?" His voice was low, but she felt the heat in it.

"Calm down. I wasn't serious. I mean, I was curious if I could get it, but leave all this?" She gestured to the deep freeze outside.

He didn't laugh. "But now you're serious."

"I don't know. I just thought—I want to be out from under my father's shadow, right? Every time he shows up at a crime scene, I feel him watching me."

Silas set his cup on the sill. "You'd really leave."

She walked back over to the board. Someone had taken a shot of Rembrandt standing on the sidewalk, probably just a random shot to adjust focus, but he was staring at the stars, something almost fierce in his expression, as if demanding answers from the heavens.

Oh, he was handsome, with his dark hair, the whiskers along his jaw, the way he oozed a sort of confidence.

Someday, Eve...

His vision of their future, delivered to her in his low voice, the way it thrummed under her skin and filled her body with desire, she nearly said yes, right there. Especially when he got to, *You'll be the head of your department, an award-winning, published forensic scientist and still the most beautiful woman I know.*

Yes, he was a charmer. A dangerous, intoxicating charmer that tangled her common sense.

Stay.

For Pete's sake.

Yes, very dangerous.

"I don't know," she said finally to Silas's question. "Maybe."

"Don't marry him."

She turned, frowning.

Silas held up his hand. "I don't mean never, although, he still worries me. He's impulsive, can't play by the rules and has his own

45

mind—"

"And since when is that bad?"

"I just think that someday he'll do something that…I don't know, really hurts you, Eve. Maybe even gets you killed."

"How—"

"I don't know. Maybe it'll be a case that goes sideways, and he finds himself in some killer's crosshairs. Or maybe it'll simply be the fact that he seems to live in the moment, without a care for the future."

"Some might call that passion."

Silas cocked his head. "Some."

"You don't know him, the real him. You see a guy who risks his life for justice, but…there's more to him." She paused. "He sees me, Silas. He sees what I want. He sees what I can be. He believes in me."

Silas shook his head. "Then go be the person he believes in. If he's that into you, he'll be waiting when you come back."

She drew in a breath. *I don't want to wait. I don't want anything to happen—*

Admittedly, that had unnerved her. Because she had, more than once, thought exactly the same thing. Like when he'd camped outside one coffee shop after another, hoping to intercept a bomber, and been stabbed apprehending him. Or when he'd tackled her father last summer, willing to take a bullet from a drive by shooter to protect him. Or when he'd followed his former partner into a shootout. Or when, most recently, he'd nearly died while rescuing her from a burning building.

I don't want to wait.

But she also had dreams—the very dreams that Rem had drawn for her.

"Let's take a look at those security tapes," she said.

Silas just stood there, his jaw hard. "Really?"

"I just need to think, Si. I don't know, okay?"

He held up his hands. "Fine. I just don't want you to get in over your head, find yourself, years from now, in a place you don't want to be."

She cocked her head. "Like where?"

He walked over and picked up two VHS tapes. "Like, I don't know. Groveland Cemetery?"

She narrowed her eyes and took the tapes from him. "I'll do this." Walking over to the machine, she popped the tape in and sat down at the workstation, turning the knob to advance the tape. She fast forwarded to the time stamp of the robbery and watched a man, gloved, and hooded, enter the back of the shop. The angle showed the back entrance and the office door. He opened it and stepped inside.

A light shone out of the crack in the doorway. Maybe the light Rembrandt said he'd seen reflected in the parking lot.

A few moments later, Rembrandt entered. He didn't have his weapon pulled, and he sneaked down the hallway, barely stopping to check the office door, now half open.

Instead, he went through to the front, out of sight.

A few moments later, the intruder appeared again, popped his head out the door, took a shot, then took off for the back exit.

"Does this tape not have sound?"

"No," Silas said. He'd come up behind her, was clearly watching with her. "Rembrandt said he saw him coming out and shot at him. This jives with his statement."

She backed up the tape. Watched again as the man stuck his head out the door, then scrambled for the back exit.

"He looks startled…like something alerted him. He barely looks where he's shooting, just takes the shot and runs."

"Maybe Stone scared him away with his shot."

She picked up Rembrandt's statement. "He clearly says he saw the perp about to shoot Booker." She looked up. "It just seems so fast. No aim, just point and shoot. And, he's running."

Stopping the tape, she popped it out and put in the next one. Forwarded it to the time stamp. It showed the front entrance, the counter, and the activity at the front of the shop.

She watched as the owner fell, shot, and reached for the under-counter alarm.

Rembrandt was already at the door, along with Booker. He sprinted out of the shot, and a few moments later, she saw him creep into the view from the back. He landed beside the owner, a towel in hand. The owner grabbed his wrist, saying something, and then Rembrandt turned to look at the front door. Booker had come into view.

A sort of horror washed over his face. It was gone in a flash, and he got up, pulled off a shot to the back, then tackled Chief Booker.

"Oof, that looks like a hard hit," Silas said of Rembrandt's tackle.

She looked at the time stamp.

Ejected the tape and put in the first tape. Scrolled to the time stamp of the perp's escape.

"Booker was already on the ground by the time our perp came out of the office."

A beat, then, "Detective Stone shot at nothing," Silas said.

She nodded. "As if he knew the man was there, and was... what, was he warning him to leave?" She looked at Silas. "That can't be right."

Silas leaned over her. "He said he saw a flash of light." He pointed to the stream of light through the crack in the office door.

"You think he could see that from the pie shop next door?"

She closed her mouth, not wanting to say the words.

"Don't tell me he had one of his famous hunches," Silas said. "Because this looks a lot like Rembrandt aided our perp's getaway."

"Maybe the time stamps are off," she said. "They have to be manually calibrated."

"And it seems that he should have seen him, coming in."

"The man was already in the office—"

"Stone walked right by it, without checking," Silas said.

"He'd heard a shot, and seen the owner go down!"

Silas folded his arms and leaned against the table, looking at her. "Eve. Be honest with yourself. Inspector Rembrandt Stone is hiding something."

She drew in a breath. "No. He…"

"Your father has said it from the first. There's something about Rembrandt Stone that simply doesn't seem right. And maybe this is it—he's a dirty cop."

"No, he's not, Silas." She steeled her eyes. "No way."

He raised an eyebrow. "Then he's lying about something." He leaned close to her and lowered his voice. "And you'd better figure out what it is before you say yes to any proposal he gives you."

Chapter 5

I'm standing in my office in the downtown building of our precinct, in front of a wall of pictures, the faces of the as-yet-unnamed Jackson serial killer.

Leo Fitzgerald is his name. I know because I've been chasing this guy for the better part of twenty years, and three weeks. Even more, I've already arrested him, already wrangled a confession out of him.

Most of all, the evidence adds up. Even if I'm the only one who can see it.

"What's all this?"

Burke's voice jolts me out of the dark places my brain has settled, namely the memory of standing at Eve's graveside, fighting the boil of fury at the thought that Leo Fitzgerald has won.

Burke walks up to me, hands me a cup of coffee. "You look like how I feel."

I glance at him. "What?"

"You were a little off the hook on Wednesday night at Quincy's. I can still feel that kidney punch." He raises an eyebrow. "Wanna talk about whatever is eating you?"

I have no idea why I might have been out of sorts three days ago, although yes, I do like to work out the kinks in my brain with a good go-round with Burke. But I'll let young Rem figure his way through that. I have bigger issues.

The first being, of course, that Eve hasn't said yes to my proposal yet. I'm not sure why, except the *I still have other things I want to do with my life*, and like I said before, I fear Florida is somewhere embedded in that statement. The frozen tundra outside doesn't help. I spotted the temperature on the TCF Bank sign on the drive in. Minus ten.

So, I don't blame her for wanting to escape. Or wanting to dive into her career.

I just don't want her to do it without me.

I keep circling the idea that, if she does move to Florida, will Leo still find her, some twenty years in the future?

If she's married to me, maybe.

The thought is a fist in my throat, and I swallow past it to answer Burke's question about what I'm looking at. "Remember the body we found outside Sonny's bar last September?" I point to the shot of Lauren Delany's body. She's lying face down, a boot print on the back of her shirt. Sources said she worked for an escort service. She's been strangled, bruising on her neck, and her clothing is torn. "Eve ran DNA on the body, and the results connected her to a man named Leo Fitzgerald."

Burke looks at me. "The guy you went after in the bar in Montrose a few months back."

Not my finest moment, granted, but to be fair, I'd just discovered that Eve had tracked down Fitzgerald's whereabouts via his tattoo and the idea he might find out, and find *her* rattled my bones.

I went into the bar edgy and unhinged and got my backside

handed to me.

"Yeah. He's slippery—and today I found out why. He's an OTR driver, in and out of the state. I think I can also connect him to the death of Gretchen Anderson."

I point to the picture of the blonde nurse I met shortly after the fight in Montrose. Deep inside, I fear that somehow my interaction with her got her killed.

But I could simply be jumpy.

The last encounter I had with Leo is burned into my mind. Twenty-three years from now, after I apprehend him, he'll break out of holding and end up in the living room of my damaged home. (Taking out the elm tree that crashed through our roof is also on my list of to dos this time around.) He will tell me that he has taken Eve (or rather, that Johnny has taken Eve) and that she is gone.

He'll be right.

I'll find her an hour later, strangled and lifeless in the barn at my parents' former home outside the city.

So, of course I'm jumpy as I turn my attention to the remains of Gretchen Anderson.

No more deaths.

Honestly, however, my trip to Helen Latsky's house has me unnerved.

I'm not wrong about Fitzgerald. I can't be.

I've been staring at the evidence of these two kills for an hour.

There is one more case I need to dig up, too.

Julia Pike.

Leo's girlfriend.

The name dings a bell deep inside me, but I can't place it.

"I remember her," Burke says about Gretchen. "Early December, we found her in a parking lot? Didn't we get DNA off her, too?"

"Yeah. Again, a match to Leo Fitzgerald." I know what he looks like, the fresh memory of our encounter, not just in my home, but before, when he got the drop on me in a future past where we ended up offshore on his trawler, part of his plan to turn me into fish bait. I wish I had his picture, or that sketch we got from Meggie Fox, one of his victims who got away. But of course, I left that in the future, along with the analysis of the footprint found on Lauren's body. He leaves more footprints in the future, and Eve and I decided it came from a running shoe.

A thought strikes me. I'm an idiot. I should have picked up Leo's shoes while I was at his house.

Burke has picked up the file on Gretchen and is reading it. "She wasn't raped, but they found his DNA on her. Friends say she was dating Fitzgerald."

I nod. "He dated both women. Both women broke up with him."

"Motive, I guess. And he knows how to handle himself, given the fact he threw down with you and got away."

He raises an eyebrow and I'm remembering Burke's earlier comment.

"I suppose you want payback for Wednesday."

"I wouldn't turn down a rematch," he says, grinning. He's wearing a gray turtleneck and wool dress pants, and always looks a little more put together than I do.

At least young me has ditched the suits. I'm wearing dress pants and a clean oxford, but no tie. And, last night at my tiny dark walk up brownstone in Uptown, I noticed the beginnings of a journal, the one that will save my hide in the future.

I grin at him. "You got it."

The one thing I love is the way this younger body feels when

I'm sparring. No wonder I thought I was invincible back then. Now.

Burke nods, then turns back to the board. "You think Fitzgerald is good for these crimes?"

"I do." I say it with more oomph that I currently feel, however. Like I said, the conversation with Helen had dislodged me a little from my righteous moorings.

"Let's get him in here and have a chat."

That's probably a better answer than the one I was mulling.

"I talked with his mother this morning. She says he was in Desert Storm. Survived an IED, but had head trauma."

"You think his trauma contributed to his reaction to the breakups? Maybe anger issues?"

In later years, we'll have more by the way of evidence—the description I mentioned, a shot of his tattoo caught on a surveillance camera as he chased down his victim.

Twenty years from now, the case is solid. I need to remember that part.

But twenty years from now, we'll also find five victims that predate these murders, buried in my parents' backyard.

This is personal between Fitzgerald and me.

I probably have anger issues.

"There's another murder not on this board," I say. "A fifteen-year-old girl named Julia Pike. His first girlfriend—a hit and run."

"It's a cold case?"

I've gone into the dusty file storage and pulled her box. It sits on my desk, the cover off, the photos of the crime scene, as well as the sketchy report sitting on the desk. "According to the report, she was walking home from track practice, near dusk, and a car simply veered off the road and hit her."

I hand him the file and he opens it. Grimaces at the picture.

Pretty girl. Dark brown hair, slender, fit—her neck is broken, her death swift. She's wearing a Minnetonka sweatshirt, and I realize this is the school district Eve grew up in.

Wait—

I take the file back from Burke and scan through the pages. I don't know why I didn't see it before, but in the report is a statement by one Eve Mulligan, best friend, after she's questioned by her father, Inspector Danny Mulligan.

A long-ago conversation surfaces in my mind, one that happened eons before the nightmare of my successive lives began.

"I had a friend who was killed by a hit and run driver when I was fifteen. I always had this hunch that Julia knew the person who killed her. But what did I know? I was a kid. And it might have been my overactive imagination."

Eve, you had good instincts, even then.

I hand the file back to Burke and he looks through the pictures. "CSI pulled a tire print."

"From an Oldsmobile. Maybe a Toronado," I say. I've already read it. "Apparently Firestone designed a special tire called the TFD for these cars. Stiffer sidewall, and a thinner tread."

"You read that."

I look at him, smile. "Or maybe I just know it. All those hours working on cars with my father in his barn."

He rolls his eyes. "Please. Your father wouldn't be caught dead with a GM in his garage." He sets the picture down. "Did you do a search?"

"Yes. Of owners of Toronados in the Twin Cities area in 1987." I motion my head toward the corner of my office. "I just printed it."

"It's a luxury vehicle. Can't be that many."

I walk over and lift the pages from the printer. "Just over a thousand."

He raises an eyebrow.

I scan down the list, a brief summary of the names of the owners. "It's probably a dead end. We can't run down every person who owned a Toronado and ask them about an alibi fifteen years ago."

The list is alphabetical, last name first, and of course I slow down when I hit the "F" category. Farmington, Fletcher, Flemming but no Fitzgerald. It was probably a long shot, anyway. I hand Burke the second page, the one that starts with the Kelloggs. "See if you can find a Rossi on there."

He turns it over and studies the list. "Nope." But a moment later, after I've scanned my list again, he says, "But there is a Latsky on here."

I look up at him. "Latsky?"

"It's not the same Latsky, but isn't your physical therapist a Latsky?"

"Yeah. Gene." Unfortunately, my only memory of Gene Latsky is in the present. Balding man, a little paunchy. Seemed friendly. But, what's more interesting— "Helen Fitzgerald, Leo's mom, married a Latsky. Nick Latsky."

"Bingo." Burke hands me the paper. "1977 Oldsmobile Toronado registered to a Nicolas Latsky."

Gotcha. "Leo used his stepfather's car to run her down." I set the paper down.

Eve's best friend was run down by the man who will later murder her. Or would have, had I not I found this.

What are the odds? Fate, thinking it will win, again.

Not this day. Not ever again.

Leo Fitzgerald is going down for these crimes. And he'll never have the chance to become the Jackson killer.

Or murder my wife. My daughter.

John Booker.

My hands are almost shaking and I steady myself on the desk. I have enough to swear out an arrest warrant.

I got him.

Now, I just have to *get* him.

Tonight, I get to tell Eve we solved the cold case. That Julia's murderer will go down for her death.

Admittedly, I'm hoping she'll see my brilliance and give me the answer I want to hear.

"So, we're on for tonight?" Burke says, oblivious to my game with fate.

"What?"

"A rematch."

"Sure. I'll kick the tar out of you any day you'd like."

He's laughing. "Oh, you wish, Stone."

"Early, though. I'm having dinner with Eve." And I can't stop myself, the ebullient sense that I'm winning spilling words from my mouth, "I asked Eve to marry me."

Burke's eyes widen. "Really?"

"I know, it's fast, but—"

"Fast, yes, but ever since the fire, you and Eve have been hot and heavy, so I guess I should have expected it."

We have?

I'm suddenly wondering if her invitation for me to stay hasn't already been cashed in.

Young Rem, you jerk. I have the crazy urge to get young me in the ring and teach him a lesson.

"Rem? Are you okay?"

I'm not sure. But I look at Burke. "She hasn't said yes, yet." I pause. "I think she's got a job offer from Florida."

Thank you, Burke, because his expression is exactly the way I feel. I make it worse, however, when I say, "I can't lose her. So…if she goes, I'll go with her."

He cocks his head. "Rem. What? *Florida?* They have alligators down there."

I laugh. "I know. But—"

"Listen. I know you're crazy about Eve. But you have a career *here*. You're Booker's favorite. Man, I could see you as chief one day. Don't give that up. Eve will come back—you know she will. Her family is here."

I'm not so sure, given the history I know.

"What if it was Shelby?" I ask. "Wouldn't you go with her?"

Burke lifts a shoulder. "I don't know, man. I like Shelby. A lot. But…I'm not sure marriage is in the cards for me. Or her. We both like our independence too much."

And now I'm the one who is shaking my head. It's well past time to break a few rules. "Oh Burke. I promise. Shelby and you are going to make it. I promise. You'll get married, have a beautiful daughter named Daphne, and you'll be wildly happy."

He stares at me, his expression darting between amused and disturbed. But I've done a good thing, I can see it in his face.

Sometimes people need to see their future in someone else's eyes to believe it for themselves.

Shelby has walked into the office and I nod her direction, mostly to alert Burke. Ix-nay on the Elby-Shay talk.

"Hi," he says to her. She nods at him, all business. She's wearing pants, a sweater, her blonde hair up in a tight bun and carries a piece of paper. "The search for the plates is back. I have the address for our winner. A woman named Bianca Potter."

"Good job," I say to my rookie-trainee who will someday be my boss. But I don't feel the words.

The sooner we find our liquor store perp, the sooner I'm

popped back to my current nightmare.

And I'm not going anywhere until Leo Fitzgerald is in custody. Until Eve says yes.

And until I know we've won.

"I'll go talk to her," I say, but Shelby frowns at me.

"I'm going too."

Of course she is.

"See you tonight," I say to Burke as we leave the office. We're walking down the hallway, out into the foyer when I spot Chief Booker heading through the massive rotunda of City Hall.

Holding his hand is a little girl, about six years old. Her dark hair is up in two cute pigtails and she's looking up at her father, sheer delight on her face.

Frankie Dale. Booker's daughter, and today in a different timeline, she would be getting the news of her father's untimely death.

I did this.

Booker sees me. "Hello, Rembrandt, Shelby."

"We got a name from that plate we ran at the scene," I say lamely as we near him.

He nods. "Good."

I can't help but glance down at this cherub version of the feisty investigative reporter I know in my day. "You hanging out with your dad today?" I ask.

She nods, and her grin is minus her two front teeth. "I'm going to be a policeman someday."

No, you're not, but I don't argue with her, because the future is hers, still unwritten.

They continue on past us, and we head out into the cold.

But in my mind is my own cherub daughter.

And I smile. Because I'm finally winning this game.

CHAPTER 6

I have absolutely no recollection of the case we're currently investigating. It never happened in my lifetime, so I'm walking into this blind as we pull up to the address of Bianca Potter. According to the cold case file, we never even pulled the plate on the shooter, so this is new to the timeline, too.

Hopefully it's only the first step in this case. Because the last—very last—thing I want to do is solve it.

Yet.

I need at least twelve more hours here. Twelve hours to arrest Fitzgerald and make my case to the district attorney.

I've changed my mind about killing Leo just in case you were wondering. I can make this case stick. I just need to leave behind the right file of evidence with my younger, and still bright, self.

But I need time. So, I can admit to a less-than-enthusiastic mood as we make our way up the icy walk to the bungalow of Bianca Potter, located on Ottawa Avenue in Minneapolis. It's a cute house, a one-and-a-half story, with an attic, the garage separate and located out back. "Maybe we should take a peek in the alley and see if the car is in the garage," I say to Shelby.

She's reached the door and now turns to me, nodding.

But we're too late. The front inner door opens without us knocking, and a woman in her late twenties opens the storm door. She's wrapped in a thick navy blue wool sweater, her dark purple hair askew as if we've woken her up.

"Can I help you?" she asks. "I was just getting ready for work."

It's around noon, and the sky is a pellet gray, a chilly pallor over the city as if its bracing for a storm.

I hope not. Leo needs clear skies and good weather to get home from his current route.

We identify ourselves and Shelby adds, "We'd like to talk to you about a robbery that took place last night."

Bianca stares at us, so much confusion in her expression I don't think it's a ruse. "Come in."

We walk into the tiny foyer. The house has hardwood flooring, a tiny front room and an eat-in kitchen. The furniture looks like hand-me downs and the room is decorated in Guns and Roses posters. She stands in the foyer, her arms crossed in front of her. "What robbery?"

"Jin's Liquors, off Chicago Ave," Shelby says. "Your car was seen at the crime."

"My car?" Bianca says. "That can't be right. My car is in the shop. I've been taking the bus for the past week because my heater froze up. You need to talk to the repair shop," she says. "Harley's on 36th and Elliot."

I'm conjuring my mental math. Harley's is just a few blocks away from the scene.

Bianca pulls her hair back into a messy ponytail as she talks. "Are you sure it's my car? My Chevette is hardly the getaway vehicle of choice."

Shelby looks at her notes, but I don't need them. "The car was a Toyota Supra," I say. "So the Supra used in the crime was sporting the license plate from Bianca's Chevette."

Shelby is silent for a long moment, then turns back to Bianca. "Just for our records, where were you last night, around 11 p.m.?"

Bianca's mouth tweaks up one side. "I'm a bartender at the 400," she says. "I don't get home until 2 a.m., usually."

The 400 is a bar on the University of Minnesota's West Bank. Closed in my time, now it's still a hoppin' venue for live bands like the Suburbs and Husker Du. I think Prince played there occasionally.

Her alibi is easy to check out, but we probably don't need it. In my gut, I believe her. We thank her and of course Shelby wants to visit Harley's.

What can I say? So we climb back into my Jeep and head Downtown, past the pie place and down the street to the garage on Elliot and 36th. The shop is located ten yards off the street, almost an afterthought in the middle of a residential area.

A few cars sit in the lot, and the three big shop doors are closed. I spot a blue Chevette and make a mental log. We go in the main entrance to a small waiting area. A thick cloud of grease and oil hangs in the air, and out in the shop area, a place separated from the main office by glass, the screech of an air drill is followed by the compressor coughing off and the clanking of metal on engine.

Four cars are up on lifts, red Snap-on toolboxes pulled up, a number of mechanics dressed in greasy overalls attending to their patients.

The radio is playing, the local classic rock station and I'm right at home with "Any Way You Want It," by Journey.

It would be nice to join them, the cool steel of a torque wrench or a 16 gauge ratchet in my grip.

I should probably visit my parents this time around.

A big man, grease on the tiny hairs of his arms, dressed in overalls and a gimme cap comes out of the office. The name Harley is embroidered in an oval tag on his uniform.

Not hard math. "You're the owner here?"

He nods and I introduce myself and Shelby.

He considers us and I don't sense defense in his expression. However, he scowls when we tell him about the robbery, just down the street. "I saw the police tape up this morning when I came in."

"The car used in the robbery had a license plate assigned to a Chevy Chevette that is parked out front. The car belongs to a Bianca Potter."

Maybe he's noticed his hands because he picks up a rag, starts to clean them. "Yeah?"

"Do you also happen to have a Toyota Supra in the lineup?"

He frowns, but leads us back into the small office where he turns to a greasy desktop, the keyboard covered with a plastic liner, so darkened I doubt he can see the keys. But he types in something and nods. "Yeah. We finished it a few days ago, parked it in the lot." He leans past me and looks into the lot through the door. Makes a sound, then turns back to the computer. "The owner hasn't picked it up yet, but I don't see it out there." He closes down his screen. "Let me ask the boys. Maybe someone checked it out for a test drive."

I look at Shelby and I can see the gears in her head whirling.

It wouldn't be hard for someone to sneak into the lot and change the plates. Even more likely is one of the employees grabbing the keys for an accessible getaway car.

Harley pushes out into the shop, and we follow. Music plays on the radio—38 Special's, "Caught up in You"—and he turns the music down and shouts. "Hey! Anybody take the Supra out for a test drive?"

I might have handled that better. Maybe talked to each one of his mechanics separately, gauge their responses, their body language. Maybe even brought them into the tiny office.

Because then no one could run.

Which is exactly what happens when one of the men—a skinny guy with a stocking cap—looks up at us. It takes a half-second and the man bolts for the back door.

What the—

And this could be easy. We simply get his name. His address. Park outside his house and wait for him.

But no, I've forgotten that I'm with Shelby. She's not only eager, but she's waited years to be given a shot at inspector with the Minneapolis Police Force, a job I'm apparently instrumental in training her in.

She takes off after him like a sprinter, turning to shout at me. "Go out the other door!"

Great. All of a sudden, I'm in an episode of Law and Order.

"Bryce!" Harley calls, but doesn't give chase.

I turn and look out the window.

The snowdrifts are deep surrounding the parking lot, and the only way out is through the drive by the front door.

Where Shelby is herding the guy.

This is way too easy. In thirty seconds we'll have caught the guy, and be careening forward in time about twenty years. At this rate I'm going to get whiplash.

And everything, all of it, will be for naught. Leo will be lost in time, and if I can't stop him in the past, I'll lose Eve, and Ashley, and there will be no rewrite of what went down in my future.

I charge through the garage and bang out the back door into the cold air. Shelby is a good twenty feet ahead of me, and Bryce is running hard toward the middle of the parking lot.

David James Warren

Have you ever run on snow? At best it's slow. Worst? Slippery, lethal and downright comical.

And, I'm wearing street shoes.

Shelby is wearing boots, but they're the fancy kind, and despite her best efforts, it's slowing her down.

"Shelby!" I shout, even as she's yelling at Bryce to stop running. We're both wasting our breath.

She slips, and her boots slide out beneath her.

Just like that, she's down.

Her shouts make Bryce glance back. And then, even as I sprint-slash-slide toward Shelby, he turns and doubles back.

"Stop!" I shout because everything inside me has gone cold. Bryce is gripping his socket wrench like a hammer, and it's big, the kind with a heavy 1 inch ratchet driver at one end.

Shelby is still on the ground, rolling over to get up. As he runs toward her, he pulls back the ratchet, looking to cave in her skull.

"Shelby!" I shout. I'm five feet away, and it's an impulse more than clear thought that causes me to dive at him. A sort of instinct that comes from the fifty-year-old inside me rather than some heroic burst from the young buck I inhabit.

I hit Bryce in the waist just as his ratchet smashes into my shoulder with a sickening crunch, and it's hard enough for me to know it's going to leave more than a bruise. We land hard—the icy pavement unmerciful and my shoulder slams into the ground.

I don't know if I've dislocated it, but white-hot heat spears through me as Bryce scrambles up.

Then, as I'm rolling, trying to find my feet, he backhands me with his wrench.

I get an arm up to deflect it, but the blow still lands on the side of my head, and the sky spins.

Bryce takes off.

And I'm an idiot in the snow and ice, blinking, trying to right the world.

Shelby is kneeling beside me. "Rem!"

I hear more shouts behind her—probably Harley and the guys from the shop.

"Call 9-1-1," she shouts, but no that's not necessary.

"I'm fine," I say and sit up, and only then notice the heat pooling in my collar.

I'm bleeding. Shelby is making a face and I press my hand to the wound. A serious welt is growing under my hand, my head throbbing.

Shelby has whipped off her scarf and now presses it to my head. "Why didn't go you out the front?"

I suppose that's a good question, but I frown at her because *really*? If I had, I wouldn't have been close enough to take that hit for her.

"If I had, you'd be dead."

She purses her mouth in anger as sirens whine in the distance.

I don't have time for this. Getting hauled into the ER will eat up hours of my day, and what if some crazy, overprotective doc decides I might have a concussion?

I have things to do. A date with Eve, Leo, and a large elm tree. Pushing to my feet, I let Shelby grab my arm because yes, the world spins, but then I shake her off. "It's just a little cut."

She looks dubious, but I turn to Harley, who is caught between a look of horror and the very real fear of what this could mean for his place of business. "I want everything you have on this Bryce—"

"Miller. Yes, of course," he says.

A cruiser pulls up and out steps a face I know well—beat cop Jimmy Williams and his partner, Jackson O'Shannesy.

Shelby gives them the low-down, and Jackson hands me a gauze pad from their first aid kit. I sit on the back bumper of the car.

Head wounds bleed. I know this. And my shoulder is screaming. But I don't want anyone tracking down Bryce quite yet so I'm not going to leave the scene.

Besides, I've been mulling over a hunch.

How did the perp at the liquor store know about the safe's location? I have a gut feeling it's someone who might have worked there.

Just to confirm, I turn to Harley. "Can we get a list of all your employees for the last two years?"

Thankfully, he doesn't ask for a warrant. He just nods and leaves for his office and Shelby asks the other mechanics about Bryce.

Officer Jimmy Williams—he's a big man, over six feet, strapping, capable, and twenty years from now he'll be shot in the head in an ambush by a fifteen-year-old gang member.

Only, that was in my timeline. More recently, apparently, I save his life in that same ambush.

Now, he comes over to me. "You okay, Inspector? You took quite a hit there."

I nod, taking the gauze away. It's stopped bleeding, but my head is still banging.

"First the car accident, and now this," he says. "You always seem to be in the thick of it."

Yes, I do, don't I? I say nothing, though and he sighs. "You ever wonder if it's worth it?"

I look up at him and frown.

He shrugs. "The wife and I are adopting a little girl. I just don't want…" He looks away. "Aw, I'm just spooked."

I get it.

I suppose *spooked* accurately describes my own impulse when I turned in my badge to Booker after seeing Jimmy die.

Or maybe I was just tired of trying to throw another sandbag against the rising tide of crime.

I nod now, and get up. No spinning, so I'm good to drive. "I'll be okay. Can you give Shelby a ride back to the station? I'm going home to get changed."

"Just stay awake, all right?" he says, still looking dubious.

I leave Shelby to gather names, climb into my Jeep and head back to my apartment. It's not fancy, just a one bedroom walk-up in the Uptown area, with a mostly bare fridge, and decorating that screams bachelor. I hate the place.

Of course, back then, or now, I thought it was cool. A black leather sofa, big plasma flat screen television and a fancy DVD player, I spent big on new equipment.

I shed my coat and shoes at the door and walk straight to the bathroom to take a look in the mirror.

Wince. I need ice, the skin broken around a dark welt in my hairline, and maybe a stitch or two.

I unbutton my shirt and ease it off. The bruise is deep, running along my collar bone and up to my shoulder. It's not dislocated, but its seriously sore.

Turning on the shower, I strip, then stand under the hot spray a long time.

I'm tired. Tired of bouncing between worlds, tired of trying to stay one step ahead of time.

Tired of playing this game, especially alone.

I close my eyes and lean my head back against the tile.

I'm tired, most of all, of lying.

I get out, dry off, slide into a pair of jeans and grab some ice from the freezer, dropping it into a bread bag and tying it.

Then I lay on my sofa and press the bag to my head.

I know I shouldn't sleep, but I do let Eve slip into my head. She's wearing a pair of jeans, her reddish hair down and she's standing at the counter of our someday-slash-now craftsman home. She's chopping a watermelon and a slight smile is playing on her lips as she watches our daughter, Ashley, swing on her new swing set in the backyard.

The one I built.

It's a memory, not a daydream, but it feels as slippery as a dream, my fingers falling through it as I reach out to her, to press a kiss to her neck.

My throat fills.

Stop, Rem. Get a hold of yourself.

The buzz at the door jerks me out of the dark spiral I can't seem to escape and I sit up.

The world tilts, and I grab the sofa before I go down.

Maybe I do have a concussion.

But I get up, make it to the door and open it.

Words escape me. Eve is standing in my hallway—she knows where I live? What have you been up to, young Rem? Her auburn hair flows out from under a wool hat, and her hazel-green eyes are hard in mine.

I hope he hasn't already started down the path of relationship mistakes, the ones I'm trying to reset. In my first go around, it took us years to overcome the fallout of those first nights.

"Eve?"

"We need to talk, Rem," she says. But her gaze runs over me.

I'm shirtless. And in my young body, and I'm suddenly aware that she's blushing.

Maybe she's here to tell me yes. That she can't wait until

tonight—and even, that she's heard about the attack in the parking lot, and that she can't live without me.

I know, I'm a sap, but I'm hurt. Give me a break.

Then her eyes land on my wound. "That looks bad. Are you okay?"

I nod, but then wince.

"Oh, Rem, what happened?"

I step away from the door, and she comes in.

"Your shoulder—" She reaches out as if to touch it, then pulls back. "It looks broken."

"I can move it." And I prove it, although I hold in a groan.

She looks dubious and shakes her head. "The invincible Rembrandt Stone."

I have no comment.

She's holding a bulky envelope and now she surveys my tiny apartment. "Nice television."

I'm doing a little fist pump because her comment tells me that maybe she *hasn't* been here before. Hasn't spent the night in young Rem's bed.

"Thanks," I say, and shut the door behind her.

She now turns back, and all the hope I have that she'll smile, take my hand and tell me she loves me, that of course she'll marry me, that we are meant to be together, dies when her mouth tightens. Then she sighs and says. "Rem, I know you're lying."

I frown, cock my head.

"I know you're hiding something from me, and before I could ever marry you, I need to know what it is."

CHAPTER 7

I travel in time.

It's the first confession that comes to mind at Eve's accusation—I know you're hiding something—and the words just spill out, right there. *I am a time traveler, Eve.* This is how I know things, how I stop things. More, we're married—or we were, and I know you. I know how you love to take off your shoes after a long day and ride in the car barefoot, and that you're a cheap and easy date on a Friday night—a ride in the Porsche and an ice cream cone under the spill of stars and I can have my way with you. I know how hard you've worked to become the top of the department, and how you're also an amazing mother, how your love for your daughter is your entire life, your breath.

You would do anything for our family.

I know how you poured yourself into finding your father and brother's killers, and that's why I came back to stop their deaths. Your mother was shot, instead, but she lived.

You won't believe this, but in that version of events, you ended up in Burke's arms, but I went back and changed that. Not purposely, but fate has decreed we will be together.

I've saved Burke's life, too, and set up your friend Shelby and him for a happy ending.

I've been back in time four times now, in this younger body, and it's not without confusion, not without purpose. And not without wanting, with every beat of my heart, to tell you this.

In my head, Eve looks at me the entire time I say this, her eyes widening, her mouth opening, but she doesn't interrupt. And when I'm finished, she puts down that envelope and throws her arms around me. *I knew something was special about you, Rembrandt,* she says. *There is no one as clever and brave as you to try and fix the past.*

I'm here to save your life, I whisper into her neck. Because you're murdered by a serial killer on the loose in the future. Then she leans back and stares at me with so much love and fierceness in her eyes that I can't help but kiss her. I wind my arms around her and pull her to myself and I am lost in her touch—

"Rem, did you hear me?"

My tiny but perfect daydream vanishes at the sound of Eve's voice and I snap back to the reality where I *don't* spill out the truth. Where I'm standing in my small apartment, a cold pack to my throbbing head and Eve is demanding the kind of answers I can't give her.

Because even though I'd love to pretend that scenario is possible, I know it wouldn't pan out that way. At best, she wouldn't walk out and call me crazy.

"What do you mean?" I ask and yes, it's a lame, time-buying question, but…what exactly does she mean by *hiding something?*

"I mean, last night in your report about the Jin's Liquor's break-in, you told Burke you saw a light flashing in the parking lot, and that's what alerted you. But I saw the tapes and there's *no way* you would have seen the light. And then…" Her mouth makes a grim line even as she shakes her head. "Listen, I really want to hear your side, here, so please don't lie to me."

"Then what?" I ask and lean against the wall because the world is still spinning a little. My skin is starting to freeze around the wound, the thump of pain muted by the hammer of my heart.

"Well, then you said that the perp nearly took a shot at Booker, but the time stamps on the two security tapes don't match." She raises one beautiful, way-too-clever-for-my-own-good eyebrow. "How did you know he was there, because you never even looked in the office when you came in. It was…well, like you *knew* he was there, but didn't care."

Oh. And *uh oh* because I see where she's going with this. "You think I purposely let him get away."

Her mouth pinches. Then, "Rembrandt, are you in trouble?"

Oh, Eve, you have no idea. But I give her a blank look.

She looks at my head, and back to my face. "What aren't you telling me?"

My heart just about explodes because she hasn't gone to Internal Affairs, but to *me*, to ask *me*. To help me cover my backside.

Because she loves me.

I take her by the elbow and lead her over to the sofa, mostly because the room is still tilting, but also because I'm stalling again.

By the time I hit the sofa, I have it. "Okay, yeah, there is something I haven't told you."

She sets the bulky envelope on the coffee table. I'm guessing it holds the security tapes.

"I do want to be honest with you, Eve," I take her hand. "But you need to…well, believe me." And for a second, I'm holding onto that fantasy of her doing exactly that. Believing me.

And the what-if—the dream of telling the truth, of her in my arms, of us becoming a sort of time-travel team, as crazy as that sounds—makes me consider actually telling her the truth.

I travel in time.

But it isn't those words that emerge from my mouth. Instead, "I get premonitions about things."

She takes her hand from mine and cocks her head.

My heart is lodged in my throat.

Finally, "I'm listening."

Please, Rem, don't blow this. "Eve, if I didn't shoot into the air, and scare that perp away, he would have come into the hallway, seen Booker standing there, panicked and killed him." I put the ice pack on the table. Her gaze goes to my head and she winces.

"I wish I'd gotten a premonition about a guy swinging a wrench at my head," I say, trying out the joke.

She doesn't smile. "What kind of premonitions?"

So, too early, then. "I can see…the future. A foreknowledge, maybe." And that's as close as I'm going to get, I think. "I just know, in my bones, that something is going to happen."

She takes a breath. "Like a hunch."

I nod, but just a little because I really need some pain killer. "I get a lot of them."

"Like when you knew that there was a drive-by shooter outside our house."

"I thought he was aiming at your dad, though," I say, hoping to add a fallibility to my hunches.

"And the coffee shop—you were sure the bomber was going to try again."

I nod. "Although in my defense, I did check out a number of them before I got it right."

"And the whole, Burke needs me, a few months ago, right before you go to a house that has a meth lab?"

"I didn't know the meth lab was there—"

"Rem! You got all those *right.*"

I close my mouth. Nod again. "Premonitions."

"Where do they come from?"

"The universe?" So lame and now I feel like the stars are watching and I'm really going to be in trouble.

Eve isn't buying it. "Rem—"

"Okay, I'll prove it." I take a breath. "You're going to get a job offer from Florida."

Her eyes widen.

"And you're going to take it."

She's just blinking at me, and I am such a jerk, but I'm a little desperate here. Because I so need her to not only believe me but see a future with me. "If you take it, you'll go down there and meet a cop named Val. And he'll do his best to charm you, and you might even fall in love with him." I take a breath and touch her hand. I don't need a hunch for this. "And it'll break my freakin' heart."

Her eyes narrow. "That's not funny, Rembrandt."

I frown, and she pulls her hand away from me. "Silas told you, didn't he?"

"Told me what?"

"I told Silas about the job offer this morning."

Oh, no—

"Did he call you?"

I'm trying to get my mind around time, and how it just keeps throwing me a jab. "Silas hates me, and we both know it."

Her mouth opens. "He doesn't *hate* you."

"Please."

Her mouth tightens. "Fine. Then how did you know?"

"I told you. Hunches. Premonitions."

I can almost see the possibilities churning through her head. But that's not the important part. What settles in my brain is that I. Was. *Right.*

"You did get offered the job."

She nods.

"Eve, I know I'll be a jerk if I tell you not to take it, so you need to know if you do, I'll follow you."

"What?" She sits back, staring at me as if it's *this* statement, more than my previous, that has completely thrown her.

"I choose you, Eve. I meant what I said." I take her hand again. "Marry me. We belong together." Fate has proved it. But I don't say that.

She looks at my hand, and when her gaze returns, there's almost a pleading in it. "All those things you said—about the house and the little girl and—"

"Your career? All of it happens, Eve. I promise."

She holds my eyes. Takes a breath. "You can't promise that."

Maybe not. After all, fate is still at the helm. But this game isn't over. "I can try," I say, and smile.

And then, she nods.

Did you see that? A nod, and now I've somehow coaxed a real smile out of her.

"Rembrandt, you are...so..."

"Handsome. Brave. Clever—"

"Dangerous," she whispers, then leans close and kisses me.

See? I had a hunch it might end this way.

Except, maybe not exactly this way, with her climbing into my arms, and us softly cocooned onto my skinny leather sofa. Her arms are locked around my neck and as I lift my head, I realize I've completely forgotten I am twenty-nine-year-old Rem.

And she's not my wife of twelve years.

She's shed her jacket, dropped it in a ball on the floor and I'm suddenly, keenly aware that I'm shirtless, and she's playing with the hair at the nape of my neck, looking up at me with a welcome in her eyes that I know.

But one I shouldn't, at least, not yet. It occurs to me that maybe we've been here before, as in young me and her, tucked onto this sofa, on our way to a place I want to keep sacred.

"Eve," I say. "Maybe…" I lean up, my heart hammering. "I think maybe—"

"I'm staying, Rem."

Oh. Wow. She pushes against my chest as she stands up and reaches for her coat, now on the floor. "Put that ice pack back on your head."

I know that now *I'm* wearing a look of confusion.

"You probably have a concussion, tough guy. And there is no way I'm going to let you fall asleep and never wake up."

Ah, yes.

Outside, the sun has succumbed to the night, darkness pressing against the windows. She hangs her coat by the door, takes off her boots, and walks in her stocking feet to the kitchen.

"You got a pizza delivery place around here?" She's opening up the drawers, as if looking for a menu. And bingo, she finds one and comes back over, and sits down on the sofa, pulling her feet up.

"How about a pepperoni and mushroom—"

"And green peppers." I add.

She looks at me.

"Hunch."

"Whatever." But she's smiling as she picks up her cell phone and orders. Then she goes over to my DVD collection and selects one.

"*Twister*," she says. "That'll keep you awake." She's kneeling in front of my machine. "How do you work this thing?"

I lean back and close my eyes, because my head does hurt, and she'll figure it out.

"Hey!"

A body settles on me. She's in my lap, and now catches my face in her hands. "Wake up!"

I widen my eyes. "I'm awake." She looks so serious I can't help but laugh.

"What?"

Now I want to weep because it so reminds me of, well, us. Of the Eve that was my partner, my best friend, the one person I could turn to.

The Eve that was my life.

And even as she's sitting there, even as I put my hands on her hips, I know.

If she stays the night here, then she will *stay the night here.* We will end up in the next room, and while there is a part of me that says, hello, *about time,* the older me is still wanting to get this right.

I don't want to implode my world with any wrong steps, anything that could derail the life I know we can have.

"Eve. Cancel the pizza." I move her off me and get up. Yeehaw, the room doesn't tilt. I might live through this.

"What?" she says. "Why?"

"Because we're leaving." I grab my coat, a hat, shoes and I'm going to stop at a hardware store.

Good girl, she's on the phone, canceling our pizza. When she finishes, she comes over and gets her coat. "Where are we going?"

My head has stopped hurting or is at least down to a low throb because I've found my footing.

The game is back on.

"We're going to cut down a tree."

CHAPTER 8

Rembrandt Stone had lost his mind.

Maybe he had before this—with all his talk about premonitions and the future he'd painted for her.

But he'd known about Florida. And he was right about Silas too.

Hunches, huh?

She'd shown up at his door ready for—well, for lies, maybe. For a flimsy defense, why what she'd seen wasn't correct.

He hadn't even given a swipe at denial. Just went straight to the story about his supernatural hunches. And, with the evidence he lined up, he had a pretty compelling case.

More, she didn't even mention the way he did seem to *know* her—from her favorite pizza toppings to her coffee and sandwich choices to even the way he turned up the radio to Journey's, "Don't Stop Believin'."

"I love that song," she'd said.

He'd looked over at her and grinned. "Yep."

If she was hoping to disentangle herself from Rembrandt Stone and start a new life in Florida, she was heading the wrong direction.

This man was serious trouble for her heart. Because, the painful truth was she would have been okay with parking on his sofa all night, nudging him awake and watching his small collection of movies on his impressive flat screen.

Or maybe, even finding herself in his arms again, cocooned in his embrace. She hadn't even realized she'd peeled off her jacket, had let him move her over, had circled her arms around his neck until he moved away.

Until he wore a sort of panicked look in his eyes.

Which again blew away all the rumors whispered about him.

And then… *we're going to go cut down a tree.*

What? In the freezing cold in the middle of January?

She'd thought he was kidding until he'd driven them to a hardware store and he *purchased an axe.*

Then he drove them through a number of south Minneapolis neighborhoods until he pulled up in the alleyway south of Drew Avenue.

The streets were dark, the deep frigid night holding no welcome as they parked next to an unattached garage, the snow piled up on either side of the double driveway. Beyond that, a tree arched against a back fence, maybe twelve feet high, given the headlight Rem flashed on it a second before he turned them off.

He left the Jeep running, though, as if planning a quick getaway.

Then he got out and retrieved the axe from the back.

"What on earth are you doing?" she whispered, her coat pulled around her.

The man looked rough in the dim glow of light given off from the back porch lights. The welt on his head, along with the scrub of dark whiskers and the black wool jacket, worn like a duster, collar up, turned him into some middle-aged warrior.

Or, the grim reaper, especially with the axe in hand. But his blue eyes held a sort of mischief that stirred to life a part of her she couldn't deny.

"Rem?"

He walked up to the tree. She'd guesstimate the trunk at maybe ten inches around. "Stand back."

She had a moment of pause before he swung the axe back, and then with a strong movement of his hips, slammed it into the base of the tree with a hollow thwack.

"Rem! Stop! What are you doing?" She backed up, looked around to see if the noise had echoed down the street. No lights flickered on…yet.

He swung again, and cut a deep wound into the bark.

"Rem, you're killing it!"

He glanced at her. "I know. But it's going to die anyway, in about fifteen years, and by then it'll be fifty feet tall and lethal."

"What? Now you can predict the future of a *tree*?"

A car drove by at the end of the street and she stepped deeper into the shadows.

Rem hit the tree again, and more wood chipped out.

"You're going to hurt yourself!"

"I'm fine. Listen, when this comes down, make sure you're out of the way—"

"You can't chop down someone else's tree!

He stilled, stood up and then walked over to her. Set down the axe and curled his hand around her neck.

Then, he pressed his forehead to hers. His voice turned soft. "This is our tree, Eve." He leaned back. "It's our tree and in about twenty-three years, it's going to come down in a terrible storm and destroy our beautiful house. But not anymore."

She looked at the house across the street, then the one behind them. "Which is ours?"

He smiled. "I'm not telling. But I'm glad to hear you believe me."

Shoot. Because, weirdly, she did. Or maybe she just wanted to. Wanted to embrace this mystery that was Rembrandt Stone.

He took another swing, and the tree shuddered.

"We need to make sure it doesn't hit any power lines," she said and moved over to it. "I'll push." She put her hands on the trunk, above where Rembrandt's strokes had chopped deep into the tree.

"Just a couple more," he said and swung hard again. The tree thrummed under her hands.

Sorry little tree. Maybe it would die—or maybe his assault on it would cause it to happen. Regardless, he believed it, by the way he chopped at the tree.

It cracked, and shivered, the crevasse in the tree deep.

A light flickered on in the back porch of the lot across the street.

"Hurry up!" she hissed.

He hit it again, and it cracked more, starting to topple.

A man appeared on the porch, dressed in boots and a parka. "Hey, you! What are you doing?"

Rembrandt looked at her, at the man, and gave the tree one more chop.

It shuddered, and a terrible crack rent the night.

"I'm calling the police!"

Eve glanced at the man even as she pushed on the trunk. He had his phone out. "Rem, we have to go—"

"It's not down yet!"

"It will be—let's go!" She grabbed his arm and pulled him away.

He stared at the tree, as if assessing her words.

"C'mon!"

"The police are on their way!" the man from the porch yelled.

"One more!" Rembrandt shook away, set his feet and swung hard.

The tree cracked, and then, just like that, it started to fall.

"Go, go!" Rem shouted and she turned and fled to the Jeep as the man on the porch shouted and headed toward them along the shoveled walk to his garage.

She threw herself into the front seat, the tree now down and blocking the road.

Rem climbed in the front and put his Jeep into reverse.

"Punch it!" she shouted. More neighborhood lights flicked on.

He turned, staring out the back and floored it.

The Jeep skidded down the snowy, dark alleyway—

"Rem, look out!"

He veered them away from a snowbank and kept going, slower.

She couldn't look. She had a hunch too—they were going to end up in a drift, trapped, and then the cops would show up and she'd be hauled down to the station and probably thrown in the clink and then her father would come and bail her out—

They shot out into the street, practically sliding across to the other side, then Rem slammed the Jeep into first and hit it.

Sirens mourned against the dark pane of night.

"Go—go!"

But he *didn't* speed off into the night. Instead, he turned down a side street, then pulled in behind a caravan, half-covered with snow, and shut off the Jeep.

"What are we doing?" she whispered.

"Hiding."

Her hands shook, and he took them in his, holding them. "Shh. Are you cold?"

"We nearly got caught!"

But he was grinning at her and she couldn't help but grin back. "Stop it," she said. "This is not funny."

"Then why are you smiling?"

"I don't know. Because—*I don't know!*" But she couldn't stop.

"You had fun."

"What—no! We broke the law. We murdered a *tree!*"

"C'mon admit it." He leaned in, his eyes in hers. "You liked nearly getting caught. That feeling of mischief."

"I didn't."

"You have a little bit of a troublemaker inside you, Eve." He winked.

"No."

"C'mon. You never sneaked out of the house?"

Her mouth opened. "That was your fault. And we sneaked *into* the house, if I remember correctly."

He laughed, something deep and resonant and it slipped under her skin and into her stupid, way too romantic heart.

"Please. You never went skinny dipping off your dock?"

"No…I wouldn't…*what?*"

He laughed and winked again. "You will."

Her mouth opened. "No…I don't care what your hunches say…I *would not.*"

A police cruiser drove past them at the end of the street. She ducked down.

"They can't see you," Rembrandt said. "They're not going to find us."

"We just killed a tree."

His smile vanished. "We just saved our house, Eve. And, in a way, our life." His gaze turned solemn. "We saved *us*."

Aw, see. There was just something almost hypnotic about Rembrandt. Especially when he touched her cheek, his thumb moving down, eliciting a thousand electric ripples.

Okay, she'd bite. "Why, Rem? What happens if you don't cut down that tree?"

She could almost see it, a rush of grief, pain, even despair that entered his gaze. He swallowed and let her go. Shook his head.

"Rem?"

"It doesn't matter anymore, because it's not going to happen."

She frowned. "What's not going to happen?"

He'd moved away, and now set his hands on the steering wheel. "I have to tell you something."

He went silent then. Too long.

"You're sort of scaring me."

He looked over. "Sorry. It's not…it's actually a good thing, I think." He took a breath. "I remember you telling me about your friend Julia Pike. About how she died by a hit-and-run driver."

Huh. Never in a thousand years would she think that he'd bring up Julia. She settled into the seat, the darkness, and studied his profile, lit by the dim glow of a nearby streetlight. Then spoke a sentence she'd never uttered to anyone else. "I always thought she knew who killed her."

"Maybe she did." He looked over at her. "Do you remember her dating someone by the name of Lenny?"

She frowned. "Yes. He was older than her, maybe by about three years. They met at a track meet, I think. He was from another school—maybe Waconia, or Waverly. Her father told her they couldn't date." She swallowed. "Do you think Lenny killed her?"

He met her eyes. Nodded.

She couldn't move. "Why—*how*?"

"You remember the case I told you about. The serial killer with the tattoo? You went looking for him at Midtown Ink?"

"Like I'm going to forget." She had a very vivid, sometimes revisited memory of Rembrandt hauling her into an alleyway and kissing her until she forgot her name, then warning her to stay away from Leo Fitzgerald, the guy with the tattoo. Sure, she'd stuck her nose into his investigation, uninvited, but she wanted to track down Fitzgerald's whereabouts.

You know, help.

Which then caused Rem to find Leo and go mano-a-mano with him in a bar in a fight that left him with stitches on his forehead. The little pink scar was just starting to fade.

So yes, she remembered very well.

"I visited Leo Fitzgerald's mother and she told me about Julia," Rem said.

She wasn't tracking. "Wait—*what?* Why would you visit Fitzgerald's *mother?*"

"I was trying to find Fitzgerald."

"To arrest him?"

He considered her in the darkness. Then, quietly. "Something like that."

It was the way he said it that raised the tiny hairs on her neck. "Rembrandt...you wouldn't..." She couldn't finish. She knew the stories of a guy she didn't recognize—stories she didn't really believe—who enacted a darker brand of justice.

"You were going to hurt him."

"I was going to stop him," he said quietly.

Silence.

"I see."

"I'm going to arrest him, Eve. For the murder of Julia Pike, and two other women."

"Lauren Delaney," she said.

"And Gretchen Anderson."

She remembered her. A nurse. Found in a parking lot outside a restaurant. Strangled. Silas had worked the case.

"Fitzgerald is supposed to be coming home sometime tomorrow." Rembrandt's voice was quiet. "And when he does, I'll be there."

She swallowed. "To arrest him."

"To arrest him."

Lights flashed at the end of the street, another police cruiser answering the call.

"We should go." He reached to turn over the car.

"Wait." She put her hand on his. The police cruiser turned down their street. "Get down."

He seemed to hide a smile as he slouched in his seat. She sank under the dash.

The cruiser slowed as it came closer.

"We're going to get caught!" she said.

His hand found hers in the darkness. "If we do, I'll tell them it was all me. You weren't a willing participant."

"I pushed the tree!"

His hand squeezed. "I gotcha, Eve. Nothing is going to happen to you, I promise."

She had nothing, caught inside his reassurance. More, his words, spoken at the apartment, slipped inside her. "*I choose you, Eve.*"

Oh, Rembrandt Stone was such an outlaw. A dangerous, mischievous, crazy, future-telling criminal.

She'd gone to his house to confront him, to give herself a reason to turn down his crazy proposal, to prove to herself that she couldn't trust him. Yet somehow, he'd stolen her heart clear out of her chest.

The cruiser passed them and slowly Rem sat up. Looked over at her and grinned. "See?"

But she didn't move. "What's not going to happen?"

His smile vanished.

"What do you know, Rem, that you're trying to fix?" She paused. "Or stop? What hunch? What premonition had you chopping down a tree in the middle of the night?"

He ran a hand across his mouth, then looked away. Said nothing.

She slid onto the seat. "Who are you, Rembrandt Stone? And why is it that I can't seem to escape the idea you are more than you seem?"

He sighed, and stared out the window, a thousand answers in the silence. Finally, he turned to her. "I'm just a man who's trying to figure out how to get it right." He took her hand. "Without losing any more people I love."

She frowned, a question on her lips, but he dropped her hand. Turned away.

And in the silence, she knew that was all she was going to get from him.

But maybe it was enough.

At the end of the street, the cruiser turned.

He fired up the Jeep. "Let's get out of here. I know just the place."

CHAPTER 9

Jericho Bloom takes one look at me as we enter the Golden Nugget, pulls out a whiskey glass, and reaches for the bottle of Macallan. "Rembrandt. I haven't seen you for months."

He's in his mid-fifties, his dark hair whitened along his sideburns, a contrast to his dark skin and eyes, and one of the most fit men I know. I first met him at Quincy's, the gym where Burke and I box. He's owned the little pub-slash-burger joint in South Minneapolis for the better part of thirty years, and the guys along the bar, including me, go here to watch the sports on the plasmas, sit in quiet and forget the day.

In my time, Jericho is gone, a good decade now, the victim of pancreatic cancer. I've forgotten how much I miss him as I slide onto a wooden stool and hold up my hand. "Just a Coke."

He raises an eyebrow, but his gaze falls on Eve and he nods. "And a booth?"

I glance around and find one in the corner, something dark and private and nod.

"I'll bring over a couple menus," he says and Eve and I take possession of the corner booth.

The Nugget is half full tonight, a hockey game playing on one of the television screens, a basketball game playing on another. Guys at the bar watch the games while a few booths are occupied with couples and a group of guys, sharing a bucket of wings and a pitcher of beer. The booths are red vinyl, neon lights glow in the window, the wooden planked floors are worn and from the kitchen the smell of grease and burgers can make a man weep after a trying day.

REO Speedwagon plays "Keep on Loving You," and it feels appropriate as Eve and I settle into the booth.

I've done it. I've saved Booker, chopped down the tree that will destroy our world, and soon the nightmare with the Jackson killer will be over before it really begins.

"I've never been here," Eve says as she looks at the paper drink menu.

"Great food—late night kitchen—and it's not a place where cops hang out, so…"

"So you don't have to talk shop when you're here. No one knows what you do, what you drag in with you."

I nod as Jericho comes over with a rag and a couple greasy laminated menus. He wipes the table and slaps them down. "Coke on the way. Special today is a blue cheese burger."

"Thanks." I don't have an appetite, but I needed a place to sort out Eve's words.

A place that isn't my apartment.

I'm treading a thin line here, and I don't want to screw it up. Mostly because the truth is on my lips, just itching to spill out. *I'm a time traveler.* But I have a gut feeling I've already stretched my luck as far as I can.

Still, so far, Eve doesn't think I'm crazy. Or crazier than usual. And, I think she believes my hunches. That fact has me thirsty to tell her everything. *"Who are you, Rembrandt Stone? And why is it that I can't seem to escape the idea that you are more than you seem?"*

Unfortunately, right now, lying seems my only reasonable escape.

I'm a coward, maybe, and fate knows it. It's part of the game—hold onto what you have in hand, or gamble for the bigger prize.

What would you do?

"I'll take the fries," Eve says to Jericho when he delivers the coke. "And a glass of the homemade root beer."

"Very good, m'lady," Jericho says, then looks at me and winks because I've brought a woman into my secret lair.

Eve leans across the table. "So, what other crimes are on your mind tonight, Stone?"

She sits under the glow of a red neon sign in the window and wouldn't you know it, but it turns her hair a deep copper. It falls around her face in corkscrews and the smile that plays on her lips, the gleam in her eyes has me contemplating all sorts of sins.

See, this is why we're not back at my place.

I clear my throat. "I think our crime spree should come to a halt. Our luck might be running thin." We passed two more cruisers on our way out of the neighborhood—clearly a slow crime night—and I drove the speed limit all the way to the Nugget. The feel of the axe is still vibrating in my grip, however. That, and the sense that it's happening.

I am rewriting all of it, and this time, I'm going to return to a life I know. A life where Eve is alive. Maybe pregnant with our child. And – please God - maybe Ashley is alive, too. The thought thickens my throat as I reach for my Coke.

"You think they'll find us?" Eve says. A cook comes from the kitchen with a heaping plate of skinny fries, glistening and popping from the fresh peanut oil, and sets it on the table.

My stomach reminds me that I haven't eaten in hours.

Eve grabs a plate and the mayonnaise in a bottle in a little rack on the table and squirts out a pile. "I'm sure the call went out over the scanner. My dad is working the night shift this month." She's added ketchup to her mix and now takes her knife and stirs it together.

I'm mesmerized because I've never seen her do this before. How is it that I can know a woman for twenty years and not realize this is how she eats her fries?

I must be staring because she looks at me, and then at her condiment. "Asher got me on this. It's really good. Try it."

Asher, who never grew up in our timeline, in the world where I know everything about Eve. I grab a fry and try her dip and she grins.

I like this new Eve, one yet undiscovered.

"Another Coke?" Jericho has swung by the table to give Eve her root beer. I lift the glass to him.

"Sure you don't want me to add a shot to it?"

In a version of me I don't like to remember, I came back a drunk, with a reputation that made me cringe. Hard pass, please, so I shake my head.

"This is a side of Rembrandt Stone I don't know," he says, his eyebrow raised, and walks away.

Admittedly, Jericho knows a number of sides to me, not many of them bright and shiny. Eve is looking at me, with questions in her eyes, so I fill her in. "I started hanging out here the year I wrote my memoir." *The Last Year*—it was more of a journal of my rookie year as a detective. "Jericho got the raw and detailed end of more than a few in-process entries. And, it's where I developed a taste for single malt Scotch whiskey."

"No whiskey tonight?" she asks.

I shake my head. "Those days are past."

She smiles, something approving in her grin, and Hall and Oats keeps tonight's theme with "You Make my Dreams Come True".

Outside, the lights off the snowy parking lot betray a fairy dusting of flakes drifting from the sky.

"I read your book," Eve says as she takes a fry, and dips it. "I thought it was…insightful." She pops the fry in her mouth. "Usually cops are these tough guys we only see from a distance. You made it real, and personal."

I'm wondering if she's talking about her father, Danny, when she refers to the distant tough guys. Maybe that's why it was so easy to woo her this time—I wasn't the guy I was supposed to be, but the Rembrandt who showed up without pretense.

A guy could say I was tired of my games of youth.

Now, I'm playing a different game. I have pretense galore. But this is my last shot, so I'm doing whatever it takes.

"I still remember the story of the little girl who was kidnapped. Your first case."

I nod, because I left out a few details. "She went missing in Minnehaha Park, but we found her body in a nature refuge north of the city."

"Terrible. And you wrote about it with such compassion."

Anger, actually.

"She was five years old. It…" I look away, and you know I'm thinking about Ashley.

"I'm sorry, Rem." Eve touches my hand. "You're a good man. A good detective."

I stare at her, a little nonplussed by her compliment. And maybe it's guilt, but Eve's earlier question, her tone of voice filters back into my head. *"You were going to hurt him."*

Yes. Yes, I was.

So, not as good a man as she'd like to believe.

And, before you ask, no I won't kill Leo Fitzgerald. There, I said it, and I mean it. Because how can I, and still be the guy who deserves Eve? Who deserves this happy ending?

Leo will do a nice long—hopefully permanent—stint in Stillwater for these crimes. And he won't be around to hurt Eve, or thirty-plus other women.

He won't kill my daughter.

I'll get it right this time. Rewrite my life all the way to a happy ending. I can almost taste it.

The guy from the back delivers a pile of glistening golden brown onion rings to a nearby table, and Eve's eyes widen.

She holds out her hand to stop the man before he can return to the kitchen. "I think we need an order of rings, too."

The cook nods, and I stare at her, then at her plate.

Eve lifts a shoulder. "What can I say? A life of crime makes me hungry."

How I love this woman. I lean forward. "So, are you going to Florida? Or are you going to stay here and marry me?"

She takes a sip of her root beer, then leans back. "Maybe I like the idea of you going with me. Us starting a life in Florida, spending the weekends at the beach. Learning to scuba dive."

Huh.

"What, Mr. Future, you don't see us turning into surfers?" She reaches for another fry.

I don't know why, but her question has me stymied.

What if we could rewrite *everything*?

What if, when I returned, I found myself standing on a beach in Florida? Would I take off the watch, like I told Booker, and throw it into the ocean?

Movement at the door jerks my attention and the what-ifs vanish as I spot Burke walk into the joint. A light dusting of snow covers his dark hair, his black trench coat, and he's walking with his hands in his pockets, easy, no reason to worry.

But I am worried. I sit up.

"Thought I'd find you here," Burke says, and of course he finds me here. He knows Jericho.

Knows me.

"Burke." I glance at Eve. She's sitting up, too. "What's up?"

He drags a chair from a nearby empty table, pulls it up, its back to us, and straddles it. "So, a weird call came in tonight over the scanner."

I casually reach out and lift one of Eve's fries. "What kind of call?"

"Seems a guy caught a couple of people trying to chop down a tree in his yard."

I look at Eve. "That sounds a little crazy."

"Very crazy," she says. But her voice sounds funny and she's wearing a blush. She'd never make it in undercover work. Thankfully the room is bathed in deep shadows.

Burke glances at her, back to me, raises an eyebrow. "The witness described a black Jeep. Didn't get the plate, though."

I dip the fry in the mayo concoction. "Unfortunate."

"Mmmhmm." Burke also reaches for one of Eve's fries. "Why would someone try to chop down a tree in the middle of the night?"

"In the freezing cold of January," Eve adds, nodding. Oh, Eve, stop. She's so red she could be wearing a sign that says, *guilty as charged.*

Silence. I eat my fry. So does Burke.

"Working the tree homicide case, then?" I ask.

"Maybe." He meets my eyes. But then he quirks a smile. "In

case you need an alibi, I have a *real* homicide for you."

"Eve and I are waiting on O-rings."

"Make them to-go. You'll want to see this," Burke says and pushes away from the chair.

"Why?"

"Because you know the deceased. In fact, you questioned her just this morning."

I frown.

"A woman by the name of Bianca Potter."

Purple hair. Guns and Roses.

The cook is returning with our plate of rings.

I'm a little slack-jawed as Eve turns to the man. "We'll need those to go, please."

The air is brisk, the temperature in the low one-digits, a deduction I make from the way my sinuses seize up when we walk outside. Burke's Integra is parked next to the Jeep. I turn to Eve. "No need for you to be up all night. Burke can babysit me."

Burke glances at me, but I ignore him. "Take the Jeep. Go back to my place, get your car and go home. Get some sleep."

She's stopped, and not a little disappointment flashes across her face. So I let Burke walk on and I turn to her, stepping close, meeting her eyes. "Yes. I can see us being surfers."

A smile creases up her face. "You sure you don't need me?"

"I always need you, Eve." And then I kiss her. Her lips are warm, and she grabs the lapel of my coat, as if to hold me hostage.

I'm ready. No ransom required.

She finally lets me go, unfortunately, and when she steps back, she shakes her head. "You sure you don't want me to hang around your place—"

"No," I say, maybe too quickly, but hello...with my body still wounded, the memory of our mutual saving of our home, and the way she tastes, a hint of salt and sweet root beer, the last thing I need is to go home and find her there, a comfort in the night.

Her smile dims but I touch my forehead to hers. "But I'll bring you breakfast."

She laughs. "Sorry, but I'm having brunch with my parents tomorrow."

"Then, I'll find you afterwards." I kiss her again as Burke calls my name.

"Stay out of trouble, Inspector," she says as she takes the keys from me.

I climb into Burke's Integra and he glances at me. "She say yes, yet?"

Technically, no, but, "She's on her way."

He laughs and we pull out and head toward the downtown area.

"Bianca was found in an alleyway not far from the 400 Bar. Apparently, she didn't show up for work tonight. The staff tried to get a hold of her, but when no one could find her, the bouncer went down the street to the bus stop, and found her body."

"Her car was in the shop. Shelby and I tracked her down today in connection with last night's robbery. Her license plate was lifted off her car and used on the getaway vehicle."

"That's what Shelby said." Burke has taken 100 over to 394, through the city, onto 35W and finally gotten off at Cedar Avenue. My gaze glances off the tall, multi-colored Riverside Plaza apartments, built in the mid-seventies, that rise and darken the skyline. In my time, the buildings have been renovated. Now, they still host the dismal peach and brown panels of a building in neglect.

Burke and I have answered a dozen or more late-night homicide calls from this area of town. Now, he pulls up to the curb just down the street from the 400 Bar, a red-bricked building on the corner. A grunge-rock band pumps out a loud clash of sounds onto the grimy street.

I get out and walk down the street with Burke. A couple cruisers splash red light onto the sidewalk and concrete. Police tape cordons off the alleyway and as we draw nearer, I realize…

I've been here before.

This is a crime I investigated, twenty years ago.

I *knew* Bianca looked familiar. I just didn't remember her name. Or… "Is Bianca Potter known by another name?"

"The bouncer called her Bee. Said it was her band name."

And ding, ding, that's the name that raises semaphores. Of course. We solved this crime. I just need to dig around in my dusty mental files and pull it up.

I spot Danny Mulligan standing with a couple cops I can't name. Danny looks good and clearly on the mend after the gunshot that nearly killed him in November. He's a tough dog, Eve's father—in my time he was gunned down twenty-three years ago by a gang hit. But I stopped that.

In this world, we're edging toward friendship.

I wonder how he'll react when he hears about my marriage proposal. I don't mention it as I step up to them.

Danny is wearing a long wool jacket, a stocking cap, scarf, gloves and he leans on a cane. When he looks over at me, he raises his eyebrows. "Burke mess you up?"

Oh, he's referring to my head wound. I pull down my hat to put the kibosh on the questions. "No. Ratchet to the head by a perp."

"You should learn to duck."

"Thanks for that."

"Burke says you know the victim." Danny gestures to the body laying out in the cold. Silas is pulling the night shift and is taking pictures while a couple more crime scene techs take samples from her body, and from the snow and grime of the alleyway. A couple dumpsters sit in the back near the entrance to the building next door, a hair salon.

"Signs of a struggle?" I ask.

"Oh yeah. She's got bruises on her face, and her hands. She fought to live."

I can't help but ask. "Did you find any money in her hand?"

Burke frowns at me. Looks at Danny.

"No."

So, not a Jackson murder. I wonder how many I've missed over the years, and am glad this isn't one of them.

"The bus stop is across the street and down a half block," Danny says. "So, we think she must have gotten off the bus and started walking toward the bar. Her attacker might have been waiting for her and chased her here, or maybe just waiting in the alleyway." He walks over to a place near the alley where a few fresh cigarette butts are scattered.

"Let's make sure Silas grabs these for DNA," I say, the memory reviving. The perp was an old boyfriend, although his name eludes me. "And ask the coroner to run a rape kit on her." I say this to Silas, who walks over to us. He's wearing a parka under his orange vest.

"She's clothed," he says, and takes a picture of the cigarette butts before he calls a tech over to bag them. "She doesn't look sexually assaulted."

"Just a hunch," I say and Silas rolls his eyes.

I know I said Silas hates me, but admittedly, I didn't expect Eve to so readily agree. Not in this time.

In this timeline, I barely know Silas.

Now, I glance at him. "I know about Florida."

He looks at me. "Oh. I didn't think she'd tell you."

"Eve tells me everything." I'm not sure why I want to pick a fight with this guy, but he's in my craw and my head is throbbing and a little white hot anger just might keep me awake.

"Then you know she really wants this job," he says. "And you proposing is messing her up."

"I'm going with her."

Silas's jaw hardens. I've always felt like he had a thing for her, and by his expression, I'm not wrong.

"Going where?" Burke says as he walks up to us.

"Florida, with Eve," I say, but this is getting out of hand. "Let's talk to that bouncer."

"You're following Eve to Florida?" Burke asks as we walk down the street.

Unfortunately, Burke's voice carries over to Danny who is reading the bus routes schedule posted on the stop nearby. He looks our direction, then joins us. "Eve is moving to Florida?"

Perfect. "No. She's…um…"

Stupid Burke is hiding a smile.

"I think you should talk to her."

Danny gives me a hard look. "What aren't you telling me, Stone?"

I hold up a hand. "I don't want to get in the middle of anything."

"Too late. I don't know why, but every time I turn around you're there. Butting into my stakeouts, showing up at our family picnics, stepping into a shootout and now…" He pauses. "Is there something serious going on between you and my daughter?"

Burke turns away. I think he's laughing.

Great. On the other hand, why not? I'll never get this chance again. "I love your daughter, Mulligan. And someday I'm going to marry her."

He just blinks at me. Then takes a breath and shakes his head. "God help me."

Burke *is* laughing and I shake my head and walk down to the bar. The bouncer is sitting just inside the door. Big man, with the right resumé. We ask him for the details and the dust in my memory stirs to life as he tells us how he found her in the alleyway, her body still warm. It's coming back to me now—she was killed by her boyfriend, a man she'd taken out a restraining order on, the one sitting in the glove box of her car.

I wonder why she hasn't driven it to work, like she did last time, and it's only then I realize that her car is in police impound, a victim of Bryce Mattson's crime.

Because I remembered the plate numbers.

Sorry, honey. Apparently, she couldn't escape fate, anyway.

The bouncer is wet-eyed and I know he cares for Bee, as do the various bartenders and a bandmate we interview over the next two hours.

Silas will get DNA evidence from the crime scene cigarette butts and we'll track the boyfriend down in the next few days from the restraining order, the DNA swab will match and Bianca Potter will have justice.

A guy named James Daggert, if I remember correctly.

It's already happened, the case closed. I'm nursing a roaring headache, so I take a taxi home.

It's nearly 3 a.m. by the time I stumble through my door. Maybe I do have a concussion, but my bed calls my name and I drop onto it like a stone.

Not, however, without ruing my words to Eve. I wouldn't have minded her being here, waiting for me. Wouldn't have minded crawling into bed with her, pulling her close, the smell of her skin in my mind as I fall into unconsciousness.

Say what you want, but let's remember that we're married in another life, and she's always been able to soothe the edgy, dark side of me that haunts my dreams after a gruesome murder.

Maybe it's because she's in my mind, but I dream of Florida and beaches and a little girl with blonde braids running in the surf.

My beeping phone wakes me, and I pry my eyes open, fish through the deep shadows of the morning and turn off my alarm.

I think I set it last night.

Because today, I find…and arrest, Leo Fitzgerald.

And however the next few hours pan out, the nightmare is almost over.

CHAPTER 10

I'm not sure why I'm sitting in my car, paralyzed. Why the sense this isn't going to end well sits like a rock in my gut.

I don't have a warrant for Fitzgerald's arrest—and that's my first mistake. But, to be fair, it was never my plan to arrest him. And, but for Eve in my head, maybe that would still be my plan.

"You were going to hurt him."

"I was going to stop him."

I *am* going to stop him. I'm not sure why, because I can still feel Eve's warm blood sticky on my hands, but my anger, my fury, has cooled.

Maybe I just don't want to be that man anymore, the one who lit a few rumors about some off-the-hook activities.

I'm a little ashamed, now, to say they were true, some of them occurring after a visit to the Nugget, when the stirring for justice found a dark place and ignited. Like after the event Eve mentioned. A five-year-old girl, abducted, assaulted, and murdered. And after we found and arrested the murderer, we discovered a pattern of abuse.

By her father. We had an off-duty after-hours chat outside a bar in Minneapolis that I'm not proud of, today. Then…

All right, I might be okay with it.

I changed when I married Eve. Or thought I did. But until she looked at me and spoke the truth in the Jeep—*you were going to hurt him*—I realized I wasn't too far from that man, really.

Regardless of whether Fitzgerald deserves it, I've messed with fate enough, and in my gut, I fear reprisal.

So, I've locked my Glock in the glove compartment. And here I sit, watching the ranch home of Helen Fitzgerald, void a real plan. Making it up as I go along.

Which is how I got myself in this mess, isn't it?

The sun is up, a glow of amber streaming across the folds of white in the yard, as if the fingers of heaven are offering me a second chance. Without the stars watching, maybe fate is asleep. I was prepared to stake out the place all day—the fact that Fitzgerald is already here suggests luck is on my side.

I'm parked down the street and around the corner, so Helen doesn't see me when she backs her car out, past the semi-truck cab parked on the side of her drive and motors away. Maybe on her way to church.

The truck cab is dirty from the miles it's put in, and I feel those miles in my body. I dare say, my soul. Everything aches, despite my youth, my shoulder now a dark purple. I might have broken something, and my head is throbbing.

I'm wearing a pair of black jeans, my leather jacket, a stocking cap and a pair of gloves. While I have my badge in my pocket, no one knows I'm here, and maybe I should have called Burke, but that would entail explaining.

As for Eve, I don't want her anywhere near Fitzgerald. Just in case—*and this will not happen*—he gets away, again.

I brought handcuffs, but I'm hoping we can just take a trip

downtown, for a chat.

Like Helen said, just a talk. Confirm his alibis.

Once he's downtown, I can hold him long enough for Eve's evidence to kick in, even if I'm not here.

And that's the crux. This must be done here, *now*, or maybe it never happens. My forty-eight-hour window is burning away with the sunshine. But everything is going to be okay, just like I told Eve, and with this thought I get out and head down the street and to the door.

The front walk and stoop are freshly swept from last night's dusting of snow and I take a breath and push the bell.

It sounds, deep inside the house, and I stick my hands in my pockets, waiting, as if, what, he's going to invite me in for coffee?

The door opens. Fitzgerald stands there, a hand on the frame. He's over six feet, with short blond hair, wide shoulders and is wearing a pair of jeans and a sweatshirt. He's got a ragged two-day beard and wariness in his eyes. "You."

I take a breath, remembering suddenly how he tried to drown me twenty-three years from now. And, with that memory come the words he spoke. *"You've been dogging me for twenty years for a crime I didn't commit?"*

The conversation about his innocence is finding its way back to me, piece by piece as he squints into my eyes. *What if we bombed a building?* That conversation included more than these murders, and we spiraled all the way back to the crime that brought me to the past in the first place.

The bombing of two coffee shops.

Leo helped construct the bomb that killed over twenty people eight months ago, a confession he gave me during our special one-on-one time on the boat.

This man sizing me up in the sunlight doesn't know what I

know, however, and neither does Eve, yet, so we'll leave that out, for the moment.

"We need to talk," I say.

He takes a breath, then shakes his head. "We don't have nothing to talk about."

Anything. We don't have *anything* to talk about, but now might not be the time to correct his grammar. "I think we do, Leo. Because your mother seems to think you have an alibi for the murders in question. She's hoping we can iron that out."

His mouth tightens, then he lifts a shoulder.

And just like that, like he has nothing to hide after all, I'm in.

The house smells of coffee, but he doesn't offer me any. He walks over to the table where a grimy fleece-lined, brown canvas jacket hangs on a chair, and pulls out a pack of cigarettes from the breast pocket. Camels. He takes one out and puts it between his lips. "So, talk," he says, the cigarette waggling with his words.

It's a surreal experience, despite how many times I've done it, to be in the past, repeating conversations, armed with foreknowledge. I know, for example he'll someday ambush Booker here, setting a bomb that will kill him. And I know he'll move his mother with dementia to Florida and continue his killing spree from afar.

But right now, he's still young in his exploits. Still trying murder on for size.

He grabs a pack of matches from inside the box and lights the cigarette, then turns, kicks out a chair and sinks into it.

I see the war in his eyes, a fatigue that ages him.

I wonder if I bear the same look.

"So here's what we have, Leo. A footprint on the back of Lauren Delaney's shirt, your DNA on her body, and a motive."

He shakes his head.

"And Gretchen—"

"Don't you dare blame me for her death." He says it quietly, but looks up at me, something almost broken in his eyes. "I loved her."

His jaw tightens and I might be turning soft, but for a moment, I believe him.

The feeling, thankfully, vanishes.

"What about Julia Pike? You love her too?"

He looks away. Takes a pull on his cigarette. "Yes."

"Funny how the women you love end up dead."

He flinches, and when he turns back his eyes are wet. "Yes, it is."

I pause, just a little nonplussed by his response. Then, "Julia was killed by a hit-and-run driver."

He nods and holds my gaze.

"By a 1977 Oldsmobile Toronado."

He takes another drag.

"Your stepfather, Nick, owned a Toronado."

"And?" Smoke curls out of his mouth and nose.

I don't flinch. "You can see why I have questions."

"It wasn't me," he says, his eyes narrowing. "I wasn't driving."

"Really. Who was?"

He takes a long pull, then flicks off the ash into a coffee mug on the table.

"Johnny."

"Of course he was."

His mouth tightens. "Are you going to arrest me?"

"Why did you fight me in the bar, Leo?"

He blinks at this, then takes a breath and drops the smoke into the cup. It sizzles. "I thought you were there for someone else."

I frown at that. "For who?"

He tightens his jaw, then gets up and walks over the kitchen sink. Stares out at the backyard. A barren clothesline tosses in the wind. "We're brothers, Johnny and me. He would do anything for me." He nods, almost to himself. "And me, him."

I don't understand. And then, suddenly, I do.

"Johnny didn't die in the war, did he, Leo."

It's just a theory. Until now, I've thought Johnny might be another voice in Leo's head, something that seemed correct out there at sea when he kept telling the voice inside to shut up.

But what if Johnny returned from war? Wasn't killed in a roadside bomb?

What if he's real?

Especially since Leo looks at me, and his face goes pale at my words. Bingo. I knew it.

"Johnny is dead." But his voice shakes, and I don't believe him. Do you?

I grab at what seems obvious. "Johnny killed Julia, didn't he?"

He turns back to the window, his jaw hard. "I think you should leave."

"I can't do that, Leo." I get up and walk toward him. "See, it's not really about Julia, or Lauren or Gretchen."

His back is to me. I have my handcuffs in my rear pocket and slowly reach for them. "It's about the thirty-eight women you *will* kill."

He stiffens.

"It's about my boss. My wife. And…" I grab the cuffs. "My *daughter.*"

I reach for him— "Leo Fitzgerald, you're under arrest for—"

And that's as far as I get before he turns with a shout and shoves me away.

Of course, he's hit my shoulder. I grunt but grab hold of him.

"Leo—just calm down!"

Except, neither of us are calm, let alone me, and I should probably just back away. My mouth, however, has a different mind than my body. "I got you, Leo. Now, or in the future, you are going down for the murders of these women."

"It's not me!" He throws a punch, and I block it. But I pay for it when my arm gives.

He backs away, breathing hard. "You got nothin' on me!"

"I have everything! Your tattoo. Your DNA. Your MO—the *twenty-dollar bill you left on Lauren's body*! Just like you did the hookers in Iraq."

He's staring at me like I slapped him.

Then, and I don't know how, but his finds a knife—probably from the sink—and lunges at me.

I jerk back, and the knife barely misses.

Tell me why, again, I left my Glock in the truck?

I hold up my gloved hands, my eyes on the knife. It's the kind you use for cutting meat. Thin, the blade long and lethal. Perfect for stabbing someone.

"Listen—if you're not good for the deaths of Lauren and Gretchen, then all we have to do is go downtown and you can explain it to us. Give us your alibi."

He backs away, against the table. "You wouldn't believe me. No one ever believes me!"

"Okay, I'll bite. If it wasn't you, who was it?"

His jaw pulses and he's breathing hard. Then, "Johnny. It's Johnny. He killed them all!"

It's the same song I heard on the boat, right before he jumped me, threw me overboard and left me to drown. So I'm not biting.

Still, I keep my tone even because nobody wins in a knife fight. "Put down the knife, Leo, and I'll listen to you." I take a step toward him, but he jabs the knife between us.

"Stop."

He's trembling, and his mother's words are swirling in my head. *Lenny came home…altered. Disturbed.*

"Okay, Leo, I'm stopped. Calm down."

"You don't understand. Johnny will never stop. He *can't* stop." He's backing up, toward the door.

If he goes through, I know—I *just know*—it will never stop. He'll get away, and even if he isn't the Jackson killer, he's connected, somehow. The killings will continue and…and I'll lose Eve for good.

So no, it's not the smartest move, but I leap at him. I slap away his knife hand, turn my back to him and trap his hand.

He shouts, but I'm not letting go of his wrist even when he slams his fist into my shoulder.

I howl, dig my elbow into his gut, but he's bigger than me and rips away.

The knife clatters to the floor.

I turn, but his fist meets my face and the throb in my brain explodes into a full out blow torch as the punch turns me on axis. Falling to the floor, I manage to scurry out the way before he lands a foot into my gut.

We're in the living room now. Grabbing the coffee table for support, I climb to my feet, again cursing my stupidity, and whirl around.

Just in time because he's picked up the knife, and I catch his downward thrust with my hands. Deflecting it away, I land my own blow. Leo stumbles, falls.

Thank you, young, virile body, even if you are wounded. Still, my shoulder is on fire, and without the adrenaline, I would be a dead man.

I jump on Leo, grab him in a rear naked choke hold that has

my legs around his body, my arm pulling hard into a sleeper hold.

He slices my forearm, and I jerk back, grunting. The jacket has protected me—it's barely a flesh wound. But it's alerted me to the fact he's serious.

He scampers away on all fours. Staggers to his feet. Turns.

The look in his eye is familiar.

This is the real Leo Fitzgerald, the one I fought in the bar. The one who kidnapped me. The one who threw me overboard. The one who took my beloved wife and strangled her.

This is the man who will kill my daughter.

He smiles. And any thought of his innocence dies when he spits, "I hope Johnny does kill your wife. You deserve it."

I go cold.

What would you do?

Fury bursts through me and I launch at him, uncaring. I slap his knife hand away even as I tackle him. We go down with a brutal crash that destroys the wooden coffee table.

He rolls away, picks up the knife again—the guy has mad radar for that thing—and launches at me.

I roll and he lands where I was, the knife embedded in the floor. He yanks it out, but he's slow, and when he turns, I'm right there with a left hook.

It barely fazes him.

He grabs me with his meaty hand, right around the neck, and for a second all I can think about is that every single victim was strangled.

By Leo's beefy hands.

I ignore the spots in my eyes, the breath squeezing out, and grab his wrist with both hands, trying to keep the knife from finding my intestines.

Instead, I sweep his legs and push.

And we're down, me with my hands wrapped tight around his wrist, wrangling the knife up, away from me.

Then, he jerks, and lets out a sound that turns me cold.

The kitchen knife has sliced through his jugular, still held in his grip, blood pooling out of him. He's staring at me, his breaths coming in gulps.

Oh, no.

I stare at him, frozen.

I did this. I step back, off him, my hands up.

But *I did this.*

Not sure what to do, I pick up a pillow and press it against his wound. Hold it there.

I could—*should*—call 9-1-1.

But I stand there, watching as Leo's blood pulses from his body, and saturates the white plush carpet. As Leo gulps for air, for life.

As his face pales and he finds my eyes.

He opens his mouth, but there's nothing, and his words are lost in eternity.

He's gone, and it's over.

I should feel something, I guess. A sense of relief, or accomplishment. Peace? Nothing.

You saved lives, I tell myself. The life of the one for the many, right?

I back up, making sure I don't leave footprints. The place is a mess, but I'm still wearing my gloves.

Then, like a criminal, I simply leave.

Close the door behind me.

Walk away, and then down the street. Get in my Jeep.

And then I drive away, into the golden Sunday morning.

CHAPTER 11

There are no happy endings.

I've know that for decades, really. It's embedded in my bones and I don't know exactly when it started, but the realization slowly seeped into my pores after watching justice derailed over and over again.

Now I sit thinking about Leo Fitzgerald's reign of evil finally being over. I should be elated, right? At the very least, it should bring a sliver of peace. But my mantra after years on the job has returned to me like a wound, thudding into my mind and for some reason driven me over to my parents' farm in Waconia.

No happy endings.

I'm sitting in their snowy, freshly plowed driveway, the sun gleaming against the grace-covered fields. White with splashes of gold sparkles. The fields are edged with pine, and the occasional oak tree, their skeletal arms reaching into heavens against a glorious blue sky. It's a beautiful day, but I don't feel it.

All I can hear is Leo's voice. "*I hope Johnny does kill your wife.*"

Then the terrible roaring in my head, now pounding with a drop of adrenaline.

I remember it now—the fall. The way I brought his arm up. The way the knife pierced his neck.

I did this.

I saved Eve.

She won't die, thanks to me, but for some reason that truth doesn't cleanse me from this feeling that embeds every heartbeat.

Shame.

I don't know why. I've had a history of seeking justice on my own and every time before this, I slept soundly. But today I'm on edge and rattled and yes, my head hurts, and my shoulder is in bad shape and for some crazy reason I'm parked in my parents' driveway, driven by a primal need to return home and talk to my father.

I'm not entirely sure why.

In my early days, we didn't have much of a relationship, their lives consumed with searching for my lost brother. But since my first jump, it's changed. We've become friends, of a sort.

Today, I think I need him. Or maybe I just need food because as I get out of my Jeep I can smell something baking.

I knock on the door and there's no answer. Then I realize their truck is gone.

Opening the door, I walk in, and the fragrance of my mother's weekly pot roast fills the room. I can imagine onions and potatoes and carrots and gravy. The tradition, as predictable as the rising sun died when my brother was taken. Apparently, it's back.

I walk over to the oven and see that it's on timer.

"Hello," I call out. The place is spotless, as usual. A round kitchen table takes up most of the room, bordered by a yellow Formica countertop and blue cupboards, evidence that they haven't remodeled.

In the timeline I just left, the house has been abandoned for years. Now it betrays my mother's handiwork—hand sewn curtains, and on the sofa in the family room, an orange afghan. The television is off, a pile of automotive magazines in the middle of the coffee table.

The house is quiet except for the hum of the furnace.

I don't know where they are, but I wonder if maybe they're at church. We were religious attenders until Mickey was taken. After that, it took a few years, but they started going again, part of their desperation, maybe, to unsnarl the grief from their heart and discover their own version of a happy ending.

I never went back.

Now, I walk out and stand on the porch, not sure what to do, but for some reason I'm pulled out to the barn. The animals are long gone—now it houses my father's vintage automotive restoration projects he putters on all winter. Standing in the door, I spot a recent addition, a VW bus with safari windows and I'm guessing it's a '67 or '68. My father has the engine compartment open in the back and evidence of him changing out something—probably a carburetor—it's in pieces on a bed of dirty cardboard.

My someday-to-be-driven Porsche 911 is also mid project, the hood open. Last time I was here, he fixed the timing belt and now has the alternator out and is rebuilding it.

All his tools are put away in his massive Craftsman toolbox, but the wooden workbench is littered with crushed cans of Dr. Pepper and empty cups of coffee.

I'm standing in the middle of the barn, amidst the smell of engine oil, old dirt and hay, and the swirl of memories when I hear the crunch of tires. By the time I get to the door, my father's vintage Ford pickup has pulled up and parked. It's turquoise blue and the bane of my mother's existence. He's walking towards the barn, probably having spotted my Jeep. He wears tweed suit pants, wingtips, a tie and a short coat. Church, I guessed it.

"Hey, son." He looks me over and frowns when he gets to the cut on my head. "You all right?"

I nod, but when he clamps his hand on my shoulder, I can't help a little grunt.

He pulls back. "You get into a scuffle?"

"I'm fine."

He takes a breath, as if he's debating an argument. Then, he nods. "Why don't you come inside and get some coffee. And, your mother's making a pot roast."

"I smelled that." I gesture to the bus. "I see you got new wheels."

"Saw her in a field, couldn't help but rescue her." He walks over and runs a hand over the body. "Has a few weak places, and the inside needs work." He opens the door and I see the bench seats are ripped, the front dash torn out.

I raise an eyebrow.

"Something to keep us busy in the winter," he says, glancing at me with a half-smile and I'm wondering if he means me. Have we been hanging out? Probably—it's something me and Mickey did before he was taken. We'd spend the winter in the barn with Dad, rebuilding something, only to sell it in the spring.

"Sure, Dad," I say. It occurs to me that's how I picked up my love for vintage rock, Dr. Pepper, and how to puzzle out a problem.

He looks over at the Porsche. "Still waiting for that belt to come in."

I nod. Silence pulses between us.

"You're not here about the car, are you." It's a statement, not a question.

I lean against a pole. "Dad. Do you ever feel God plays games with our lives?"

He looks at me and frowns. "That's the wrong question, Rem."

I frown, now, too. "What do you mean?"

"That question stems from an incorrect perspective that this life, this world, everything we're doing is the end game. But it's not. It's just the first quarter. This is just the training ground, the beginning of so much more."

I walk over to my Porsche. It's good to see her. I open the door and slide into the seat. "So what is the right question?"

"Why."

"Because I…it just feels so…well, like I'm never going to get it right."

"Rem. *Why* is the question."

I look at him.

"Consider this. God has an eternal perspective, eternal goals, eternal time to spend getting us there. And everything that happens to you, and everything you do is part of that journey to the man you'll be. What we do here is just the external activity so that God can get at the inside of us, and root out whatever it is that we're struggling with."

I stare into his eyes, not sure where to start.

He gathers up his empty coffee cups. Tosses them into a nearby barrel. "It's injustice. That's what's stuck in your craw."

"What?"

"You struggle with the injustice of it all." He picks up a rag and wipes his hands. "You have, ever since Mickey went missing."

I sigh, get out of the Porsche. Because he's nailed it. "There are no happy endings." I'm not looking at him when I say it, but hear him take in a breath.

"Rem. Your very statement presupposes that death is the end. And it does feel like the end if you have no faith, or hope. But God is just, and this isn't the end. Our job is to just be stalwart."

I jerk my head up and stare at him, the word dropping through me like a stone.

The word from the back of the watch, the one that seems to be haunting me. "*What did you say?*"

I'm blinking at him. And my hand moves to my watch, to where it's ticking on my wrist.

He walks over to the door of the barn, stares at the house. "There is nothing or no one who will replace your brother. His death forever changed me, but it made me realize that, despite the fact I have no control over who is going to hurt my children, and whether or not the killer got justice—it's not up to me. My job is to rightly handle the job he's given me."

He turns and looks at me. "Rem, did you do something you think has messed up your life?'

It's weird how my father can see right through me to my core.

"No," I say with surety. "I haven't." In fact, I've done something that should have been done a long time ago. I say it, I wish it, and yes, I agree with it. Leo Fitzgerald is dead and I've saved thirty-eight lives.

But maybe he's right. It's not justice. It was vengeance. And we all know it.

"Our job in life, Rem is just to stand firm on what we believe in. Because we are only accountable to the men we are called to be. And yes, sometimes life feels like a game because God is doing things in our lives to change us, to grow us, to get at the core. But it's not a game. And if we can just stop trying to control the outcome, you might discover an ending that is better than happy."

He turns back to the door. "C'mon, let's go inside. It's getting cold out here and I really want some pot roast."

Me too. I follow him across the yard, up the porch, and inside. As I work off my shoes, I see my mother standing in the kitchen, hot pads on her hands. She's wearing a dress, her hair pulled back.

"Rembrandt!" She walks over and kisses me on the cheek. She looks good—the same version of the woman I saw last time. Healed, strong. In my first life, the only life I really know, she had a stroke after they discovered my brother's remains and her life was destroyed yet again.

But I stopped that tragedy, and now she's better, and cooking. I spot fresh rolls on the counter next to the pot roast and a bowl of carrots and potatoes.

My stomach roars to life. Maybe that was my problem—I was just hungry. Yeah, sure.

I notice three plates at the table, and I'm about to remark that it's because she saw my Jeep. But then she goes to the cupboard and pulls out another plate. "Will you be staying, Rem?"

I frown. "Yes."

She adds my plate, a fork, a knife and a napkin to the table on top of a place mat. "Oh good." Then she turns to me. "Go wash up, and then call your brother down for dinner."

I still, staring at her. "What?" My body goes numb as my mind spins. "My brother?"

"Yes, your brother." Mom laughs. "Leonardo went upstairs as soon as we got home. I'm sure he's playing with one of those Lego sets. You know how he gets so obsessed with those."

I do?

And who is Leonardo?

My father is acting like nothing in the world has happened, but my heart has stopped because, well, does this feel like we just dropped into the Twilight Zone to you, too?

I head upstairs, every few boards groaning with my steps. The house has three bedrooms. My parents, mine and the one that formerly belonged to Mickey, named Michelangelo. I'm not sure why my parents had a penchant for giving their kids the names of the great artists. Maybe they were trying to instill in us something of destiny.

I notice Mickey's door, the one that always remained closed throughout my childhood, is open.

I nudge it further, and I see a boy, maybe ten years old, wearing jeans and a sweatshirt, sitting on the floor of the room, and in front of him is the most intricate looking Lego set I've ever seen.

I can't move.

He's got brown hair, blue eyes and he looks so much like the brother I lost, I can't breathe. There's a fist around my chest, squeezing.

He looks up at me then. "Hey, Rem." He grins. "I'm trying to figure out this new set Mom and Dad gave me for my birthday. Want to help?"

He says it causally, like we've known each other our entire lives. I walk in and sit down on the floor. Pick up one of the pieces he's locked together. "I have no idea how to make one of these."

"That's okay." He hands me the directions. "You have to find that piece there to connect these two body parts." He points to some random joint. But I'm my gaze is glued to him because he even *sounds* like Mickey.

I'm traveling through time, yet again.

The room is of course void of anything of Michelangelo's—his Minnesota Vikings posters, the football he kept on his dresser. Instead there's a Mighty Ducks poster, and some hockey equipment—a stick and a couple trophies—on his dresser, a computer on the desk.

Michelangelo has been replaced by this look alike stranger.

I set the directions down, pick up a few pieces, and make a lame attempt to put them together, but my hands feel like they've been shot up with Novocain.

"This will be fun to work on together."

"Mom says dinner's ready, Leonardo," I say, trying out the name.

"Oh, okay." He sets down the Lego pieces, gets up and heads downstairs.

I walk over to a picture propped on the dresser. It's of him, my parents, and me, when I graduated from the police academy seven years ago.

He looks about three years old..

Fate is changing the rules again.

And clearly, it's way, way ahead of me.

CHAPTER 12

She so wanted to say yes. To everything.

Eve pulled into the driveway of her parents' lake shore home, the snow piled high in a berm along the edges, the sky brilliant blue overhead.

Yes to Florida.

Yes to Rembrandt's proposal.

Yes to the future he'd envisioned for them.

She got out, her father's pickup parked next to hers, and her mind couldn't help going back to last summer when Rembrandt had saved her father's life.

"I get premonitions about things."

His words, spoken before they chopped down a perfectly healthy tree, before he told her that said tree would destroy their future home, had nudged to realization something inside of her she hadn't expected.

She believed him.

It was more than just the evidence—which he'd cataloged for her. It was his tone, the way he looked at her, unflinching. He believed it with everything inside him, and if he wasn't crazy …

then she had to believe as well. He seemed older, wiser than his twenty-eight years, and the sense of surety he possessed wheedled through her, too.

Yes, she believed him. And when he'd met her eyes in the parking lot, before leaving with Burke, and whispered, *Yes, I can see us being surfers*, she'd made her decision.

She would take the job in Florida. And would ask Rembrandt to go with her.

Not a yes to his proposal yet, but…maybe.

Now she just had to tell her parents. Namely, her father.

Yes, this would be fun. But her father had held it together when she became a CSI. And, even after she'd confessed to dating Rembrandt.

That conversation happened after Danny had been shot in the leg a few months ago, after she'd followed him to the hospital.

After Rembrandt had shown up to check on him…and her.

Why is he here? She could still hear her father's question after he woke up, post surgery, and saw Rembrandt standing by the window, out of the circle of her family, but close enough to show he cared.

Because he cares about you, Dad, she'd said. And then Rembrandt came up and slipped his hand into hers.

Because I care about your daughter, he'd added.

So maybe she could attribute his so-called calm to the fact he'd been on morphine. But he'd just leveled Rem with a look that seemed more like a warning, and then offered a jaw-gritted nod.

She climbed the front steps. This could go well.

In fact, she'd even seen Rembrandt's memoir on her father's desk recently.

Her father would like Rembrandt if he gave him a chance. Eve knew it.

She just needed to handle the conversation correctly. Wait until her father had enough coffee in his system.

Maybe she'd tell her mother, first.

Easing the front door open, she stepped inside, greeted by the smell of muffins in the oven, the sound of her brother's conversation. Sams was here, her younger brother wearing a thermal and jeans, sitting at the counter, sipping on a cup of coffee. Good. She'd talk to him about updating her laundry room. Asher came down the stairs, wearing a hood up over his long hair.

"Hey sis," he mumbled.

Their weekly Sunday brunch had become a thing after their mother was shot last summer, a way for her mom to get them all under one roof at least once a week. Too bad Lukas was in Chicago, finishing his law degree, and Jack, well, who knew where the Navy had taken her corpsman brother.

"Hey," she said and followed him into the kitchen. Her mother stood at the counter, wearing oven mitts, talking with Sams about her ideas for a back patio.

Sams, the family contractor, had just started hiring out for other jobs after finishing her back deck this fall.

She walked over to her mother and gave her a hug. She couldn't imagine her mom not being here to keep their family organized, fed and connected.

"Everything okay?" Bets asked and caught her arms.

Eve frowned, nodded, and when the oven timer buzzed, she took the hot pads from her mother and pulled out the casserole, setting it on the counter.

Sams had gotten up and walked over to the table. Picked up the Sunday paper on the way.

Her mother handed Eve a knife and she stared to cut the casserole. Her mom put the blueberry muffins into a basket.

"Okay, spill it," Bets said, glancing at her.

Her mother wore her curly dark red hair down, a pair of jeans and a dress shirt. Probably, she'd already been to early mass, waiting for Danny to return home from his night shift.

"What?"

"You are unusually quiet. And you haven't roped Sams yet into another home project."

"I just got here."

"It's true," Sams said from his place at the table, not even looking up from his paper.

"Fine. I need my laundry room done." She lifted the egg bake pieces from the pan, onto a platter. Glanced at her mother.

Bets hadn't moved, one eyebrow up.

"Fine." She turned away and headed to the pantry, opened the door and walked inside.

Her mother joined her, pulling the door shut. "I have a feeling this is going to be fun."

Eve folded her arms. "I just…how did you know Dad was the one?"

"Oh." Her mother pulled the door shut. "We're having *that* talk."

Eve held up a hand. "I'm just thinking."

"Research. I get it. Okay." She leaned back against a shelf. "Well, first, you have to know that he won't stay the man he is today. He'll change and grow, and hopefully, he'll be a better version of himself."

"But how do you *know* he'll be better?"

"You don't, but there are clues. How he treats his mother. How he treats you. The vision he has for the future. But most of all, his character. Who he is on the inside. That won't change. It'll just deepen."

Her mother spoke quietly. "This is about Rembrandt, isn't it?"

"Maybe."

"For the record, I like him." She reached past Eve and picked up a stack of napkins.

"He asked me to marry him." Oh, and she didn't know why she'd admitted that, but this was her mother. "Don't tell Dad."

Her mother sighed. "I can give you forty-eight hours. But after that, all bets are off. You know I can't keep things from your father, even if I try. He can see right through me."

Funny. It seemed that Rembrandt could do the same. It was uncanny the way he *knew* her.

"I guess it all boils down to one thing," her mother said. "Do you trust him?" She held up the napkins. "Alibi."

Then she pushed out of the pantry.

Did Eve trust him?

She wanted to. What did that mean, exactly?

Trust him to save her life? Yes.

Trust him to make good decisions? Probably.

Trust him to keep her out of trouble...hmm.

Eve followed her mom out of the pantry and discovered that Asher had carried the dishes to the table.

Her gaze went to the window, to the icy surface of the water, the snowy pile on the dock, and Rembrandt's words drifted in, wound around her.

You never went skinny dipping off your dock? A mischievous smile. Then, You will.

Shoot, but she believed him about that, too. Because an errant part of her had always wanted to sneak out in the middle of the night and dive into the lake, naked.

Maybe she didn't want him to keep her out of trouble.

Oh boy.

Eve grabbed a bowl of fruit from the fridge.

"Where's Dad?" she asked as she sat down.

"He had to work a little over. Had a homicide downtown he's wrapping up." Her mother sat at her place at the table, but in the wake of her words the back door opened and Eve looked up to see her father entering the house through the garage. He stamped off his feet, unwound his scarf and pulled off his wool coat.

Bets got up to greet him.

He kissed her and walked in, glancing at Eve. "Glad to see you made it."

"Oh?" She raised an eyebrow.

He slid into his seat at the end of the table. "I just thought you might be sleeping in after last night's great adventure. This looks delicious, Bets."

"My adventure?"

Her father reached for the basket of muffins. "Blueberry?"

"Dad."

He put the muffin on his plate and reached for the eggs. "I talked with the homeowner, by the way. He says he was afraid the tree would someday fall on the house, so he wasn't going to press charges, but…" His mouth was a grim line.

Eve froze.

"What are you talking about, Danny?" Her mother asked and handed Asher the bowl of grapes. He seemed to be waking up, his gaze on Eve, a slight smile on his face.

"Eve had a little adventure last night with Rembrandt Stone, according to the rumors down at the station."

Her mother looked at her. "What kind of adventure?"

"Eve and Rembrandt chopped down a tree in the middle of the night."

Eve took a muffin, her appetite lost. "I…we…"

"A tree?" Sams asked. "What? Why?"

"It was diseased," she said lamely. Then looked at her father. "How did you know it was us?"

"I didn't. Until now. But the neighbor said he saw a Jeep, and described both you and Rembrandt, as well as grabbed a partial on the plate. It wasn't hard to put it together."

She took a long sip of coffee.

Her father put down his fork. Met her eyes.

Everyone went quiet.

"He told me last night he was going to marry you." Her father wasn't smiling.

She swallowed. "Dad—"

"Did Rembrandt Stone ask you to marry him, Eve?"

No wonder he had a high record of confessions. She took another sip of coffee. Set it down. "I'm moving to Florida."

No one spoke. She looked at her father. "I got a job offer, and I'm taking it."

Her father's chest rose and fell. "That doesn't answer my question."

"Rembrandt says he'll go with me."

Her father clenched his jaw. He reached for the salt and pepper, and added it to his eggs.

Picked up his fork.

"Dad?"

"Do you want to marry him?" He met her eyes again. His were glossy, something in them she couldn't place.

"I love him," she said quietly.

"Does he love you?"

She nodded.

He sighed again. Looked at Bets, then back to her. "I just have two questions for you, Evie Bear."

Oh, she was in trouble when her father pulled out her nickname.

"The one thing I can say about your mother is that she makes me a better man, every day. Does Stone make you a better woman?"

She nodded. "I think so."

He blew out a long breath. "Okay. Then, second question, do you trust him?"

She glanced at her mother, who shrugged.

She was about to nod when her cell phone rang from her jacket pocket. She got up and retrieved it.

Silas was on the other end. "I know it's your day off, Eve, but we have a homicide reported out your way, in Montrose. My team is still processing last night's murder downtown and I was wondering—"

"I'm on my way."

"I'll send a couple techs out to meet you."

She hung up. Turned to her family. "I need to go." But she met her father's eyes. "Yes, Dad. I trust Rembrandt Stone. He might sometimes act a little off the hook, but that's just because he's a great investigator and doesn't always follow the rules. He's a good man." She touched her chest and looked at her mother. "In here, he's a very good man."

Her father considered her, then, "No more breaking the law with him, okay?" He didn't smile.

"I don't know what you're talking about." She grinned and headed out the door.

Technically, the homicide was located outside of their jurisdiction, so she called Silas back when she got in the car.

"Apparently, the mother of the victim says her son was being stalked by a Minneapolis police officer. She didn't know his name, however, just a description. The Montrose police called us. Plus, I guess the crime scene is a mess, so they wanted our help."

"Any guesses on the cop harassing him?"

"Dark hair, good looking, young," Silas said. "Know anyone like that?"

Shoot. "Not a clue."

A pause. "Right. Well, as soon as I get untangled from here, I'll be there. I sent a team already—they'll meet you there."

She hung up and followed his directions out to the house, a tiny ranch just outside the town of Montrose in a little subdivision. Pulling up behind three local police cruisers, she spotted a woman on the porch, talking with a female officer. She was dressed in a long puffy jacket and dress boots but looked like she'd been crying.

Eve grabbed her camera and a tape recorder and got out of the car. As she approached them, she identified herself.

"I'm his mother," she said, clearly distraught. Her hand pressed to her mouth. "He killed him, I know it."

A cold finger tracked down Eve's back. "Ma'am. What is your son's name?"

"Leonard Fitzgerald."

Leo. Fitzgerald.

Oh. No. *Rembrandt, what have you done?*

She went inside, ignoring the thunder of her heart, hearing their conversation in the truck.

Fitzgerald is supposed to be coming home sometime tomorrow. And when he does, I'll be there."

To arrest him.

He'd made that clear. But she also remembered the reason. *For the murder of Julia Pike, and two other women.*

For Julia Pike. Her best friend killed by a hit and run driver when she was fifteen.

133

If the man had killed three women, no doubt he had other ideas about being arrested.

Whatever had gone down, it wasn't without a struggle. Wood splinters scattered the room from the destroyed coffee table, a wall bore a hole from an overturned chair, and in the middle of the room a man in his early thirties lay in a pool of blood.

A tech was taking the victim's picture and Eve walked over to him and crouched beside the body. "Looks like he bled out."

"He's holding a kitchen knife," said the tech, a woman in her mid-twenties. She wore her dark hair pulled back and a yellow CSI jacket from the Minneapolis Police Department. "It looks self-inflicted, although there was definitely another person here." She indicated a bloodied sofa pillow nearby, out of reach of the victim. "So, I don't think we can rule out homicide."

Oh, Rem, what did you do? Eve couldn't breathe.

The tech took another picture. "The mother said she came in and tried to revive him, but he was already gone."

"Make sure you get shots of the kitchen area. And dust it, too," Eve managed.

The tech nodded.

She got up.

The killer had tried to save him. So, that said accident, or at least, unintentional.

The kitchen table had been upended onto its side. She spied a water glass on the floor, broken.

Maybe it had started in here.

She turned to survey the room and her gaze landed on the fridge.

A Post-It-note with a telephone number was stuck to the surface. She walked over and read the number.

And the chill spread through her entire body.

Rembrandt's number.

She lifted her camera. Took a picture.

Then she reached up and took the Post-It-note from the fridge and shoved it into her pocket.

CHAPTER 13

I need to leave before I screw this up.

Admittedly, however, I'm stuck in a Cleaver-esque version of my family that I never thought possible.

We're fixed. Healed.

Okay, not entirely because it's not really Mickey at the table next to me eating a pot roast and telling me about his recent hockey game but…

The kid looks like Mickey. Sounds like Mickey. And laughs like the Mickey I knew. The sound of it rouses an old, rusty memory that serrates pieces of me as it comes to life.

I'm not sure how this rewrite happened, but even though it feels strange and not quite right, I'm not going to argue.

"So, have you caught any bad guys?" Leonardo (I can't call him Leo) asks. I'm watching him sop up gravy with a homemade roll.

Just like Mickey.

It takes me a second, then, "I'm working a robbery case." I don't tell him about Leo and skip right over to, "A guy stole a car right out of a repair shop and used it to commit a crime."

Leonardo looks at me with a grin. He's missing his cuspids on either side. "Did you find him?"

"My partner is tracking him down."

He finishes his bread and reaches for the pie Mom put on the table.

"Not until you finish your carrots," she says, catching his wrist.

I could have told him that. I, however, finished *my* carrots and grab the plate that holds the lemon chiffon pie. It occurs to me as I dive in with a fork that this is the kind of pie I was eating with Booker, two days ago, around 10 p.m. when I jumped into now, and I'm wondering if it's a deeply embedded craving.

My father has the Sunday paper open and pulls out the funnies for Leonardo, folding it over. "For later," he says and glances at me.

There's a kindred spirit in his look, and my throat thickens because he's right.

Mickey loved the funnies.

I need to leave before I can't breathe or break out into weird, uncontrollable sobbing. Because it's so much like the life I knew, the life I longed for—

Fate is simply cruel. Because I won't remember this rewrite, will I? Or maybe I will because small memories crumble back to me, flitting in at odd times. Like when I saw Ashley's dead body while in the morgue.

But mostly, I'm in the dark.

I'm hungry for this version of my past.

"Coffee, Rem?" My mother asks and gets up to pour me a cup. I'm doing the math. My mother must have given birth to Leonardo when I was nineteen, out of the house and seven years after Mickey died. In this new version of time, Mickey's body was found immediately, so there wasn't the same waiting, the same searching, the same grieving.

That puts my mother at forty-one when she had Leonardo. Just like Eve. So apparently, things can turn out okay.

If I can fix it.

But most importantly, my mother is *happy*.

And my father is humming, I think it's a hymn from today's service.

And my world is put right.

Maybe it's a sign I've done it. Fate, thanking me for resetting the world, balancing the scales of justice. So, maybe not cruel. Maybe this is my reward.

I'm eating the pie, drinking coffee and about to ask my father how the Vikings did this year (trying to make casual conversation) when my phone rings.

I pull the phone out of the pocket of my jacket, hanging on the hook in the entry way.

Shelby.

"Hey."

"I found him, Rem."

"Are we working today?" I check my watch. It's nearly 1 p.m., and my mind goes to Eve and her brunch.

"I am, and so are you. Bryce Mattson is on his way, right now, to a monster truck rally."

"A what?" I'm standing in the doorway to the kitchen. Leonardo has finished his carrots and is now digging into the pie.

The deja vu could kill me.

"Monster trucks. You know—big wheels, lots of mud?"

I run a finger and thumb across my eyes. But the fact is, maybe it's time I get out of here before I make any mistakes. I've had a good run through the past, and as soon as I apprehend Bryce, I'm home.

The nightmare is over.

"Where?" I ask.

"The Metrodome, downtown. I'll meet you there." She hangs up and I stand at the door and hesitate, just snapshotting this moment.

I meant what I said to Booker. I'm throwing the watch into the lake the instant I'm back.

No more trips to the past. No more messing with time. I'll just have to try to solve the cold cases and find justice the old-fashioned way.

I need to get moving but I can't help walking over to Leonardo first. I slide onto my chair and turn to him. "Hey, bud. I gotta go."

"Catching a criminal?"

"Yep. But…" And I look at my father, his words in my ears. *My job is to rightly handle the job he's given me.* "I just want you to know, that if you ever need me, you just say the word, and I'm here, okay?"

There's a solemnness in his eyes that seems to understand me. "Okay."

I don't know why, but something inside me shifts, and I hadn't realized I'd been holding my breath until this moment.

It could be that I've been holding it for years.

I clamp him around the neck, squeeze, then tousle his hair and get up. My mother hugs me at the door and pats my cheek. "You be careful now."

My father has gotten up, also and walks me out to the porch. "You might need to get that shoulder looked at."

"I'll be fine," I say and shake his hand.

It feels strange, this goodbye. Because when I return, they'll still be here.

I hope.

My gut twists just a little as I walk out to the Jeep. Dad raises a hand to me, then goes back inside.

I back out and turn on the radio. Eddie Money is singing "Take Me Home Tonight", and I beat out the song on my steering wheel.

I'm ready.

The roads are clear and I make it downtown easily, hitting all the green traffic lights until I near the Metrodome. I pull up into police parking, and put my pass on the dash. A phone call to Shelby, a show of my badge, and I find her waiting for me on the second level, near section C, a couple security guys with her.

"He's supposed to be in row thirty-eight," she says. She's wearing a pair of running shoes, jeans and a short parka. "I tracked down his address from the information the garage owner gave us. He lives with his mother and she found his ticket receipt in his disaster of a room."

"Good job, Shelby."

She takes a look at my head, and says, "We'll get him this time, Rem."

But I don't need payback. I'm full up with my quota for vengeance at the moment.

We enter the arena and the place is already loud, a packed stadium cheering as five massive trucks roar through the mud in the center of the arena. Their engines are amplified, and they tear over berms, launching into the air, falling hard on their massive tires, bouncing, then righting themselves and spraying mud into the stands.

The crowd loves it.

Two trucks, one that wears a Superman cap, the other green, with a fire streaking out of the back, roar around the perimeter.

I admit, I don't understand this sport. But I suppose it evokes the same adrenaline that being in the ring at Quincy's does. A little fear, a little grit, a lot of daredevil.

The majority of the crowd are kids, clapping, holding miniature trucks, duplicates of the ones tearing up the mud.

"Shelby!" I shout over the roar in the arena and she glances back at me. "Let's try to keep this on the D-L. We don't want to freak out the families."

She nods, but I'm not sure if she can hear me because the name of a new truck is announced, to the roar of AC/DC's, "You Shook Me All Night Long".

I spot Bryce even before Shelby points to him. He's wearing a T-shirt, a full sleeve of tats, his hat on backwards as he stands to cheer. He's about half-way down the row, and fifteen rows up from a barrier that edges the oval and mud.

So, the guy put out for good seats.

I'm not sure how Shelby will play this, and I immediately see a flaw in her plan—namely, she put all her heavy artillery on one side of the aisle. There's nothing stopping Bryce from bolting out the other side.

Except for me.

I turn and take the stairs back up to a walkway about ten rows up. Run along the edge to the other aisle.

Turn down. I see her talking to the people between her and Bryce. A couple moves out, and then two more people.

It's then that Bryce spots her. I'm ten rows away, hustling fast, but he doesn't see me.

I knew it—he bolts the opposite direction, pushing people aside and heading down the row away from Shelby. She's using her manners but fighting to follow him.

He hits the aisle.

Turns.

Hey, buddy. I sprint toward him. "Bryce!"

I catch this guy, I go home.

He races down the aisle and breaks into a run, but hello, where's he going to go? Below, the two trucks have been joined by four more, all screaming around the perimeter, kicking up mud, maybe some interlude performance like they might at a rodeo.

Bryce is headed right for the edge.

"Stop!" You idiot, I want to add, but I'm breathing too hard.

Bryce hits the railing, turns to look at me. And that's when Shelby, behind me, breaks free of her row. "Police! Stop him!"

Monster truck rallies are attended by red-blooded, law-abiding Americans with families.

Bryce isn't going anywhere. And he knows it when a couple good Samaritans reach out for him.

He broadcasts his intentions in his eyes when he shoots a wild look at me, then back at the arena.

He's going over.

I launch myself at him, just as he gets a leg over the edge. Grab at his body, miss and then his grip his arm as his weight flings him over.

"Stop!"

I'm leaning over, two hands on his arm, and he's kicking to get away from me. Around me, the roar of the engines fills my brain, but I'm not letting go.

Someone screams, and I look over and see one of those crazy trucks headed for Bryce.

For me.

It hits the breaks, but with those giant wheels, he's bouncing, careening toward us.

Now Bryce has his hands on me, trying to get up. But his weight has pulled me over, and while I feel hands on me, holding me back, Bryce is wrenching my arms.

And I only have one good arm.

Pain screams through me, as he wrenches my shoulder, and I can feel my grip fading.

"Hold onto me!" I yell, but his grip is fading too. He's kicking at the boards, but it only weakens me. That's not helping, dude—

It happens so fast, I need to replay it in my head to get it all. But you guessed it.

His flailing rips him from my hands.

He falls.

Worse, he's pulled me over with him, and now I'm hanging by one arm from the railing. My shoulder is screaming.

Below me, that stupid monster truck swallows him up.

One of the tough guys in the front row reaches down and hauls me up as if I weigh nothing, and I crumple on the stairs, trying not to howl.

My shoulder is dislocated, I know it. But worse, the tragedy is playing out on the big screen where the monster truck has bloodied the mud.

In a nearby row, a woman has picked up her four-year-old and is hiding his eyes.

Horrified screams pulse through the traumatized crowd, and I'd be more than fine if time picked now to take me back. After all, despite the outcome, he's been caught, right?

But I'm still here.

Shelby has made it down to me. She takes one look at my arm, hanging stupidly from my shoulder, and calls for an ambulance.

But of course, the ambulance they need isn't for me.

A glance at the jumbotron has an EMT crew driving out into the muddy track.

"You'd better get down there," I say to Shelby. "Find out if he's alive."

And still, I haven't jumped.

"And you'd better get to the hospital."

"I can drive myself."

"Hardly. You have a stick shift."

Right.

I get up, my teeth gritted. "That could have been handled better." I don't mean it as a reprimand, at least most of it.

She takes it though, nodding. "I'll call Eve," she says and picks up her phone. I put out my hand.

"I'll take an Uber."

She frowns. "A what?"

Whoops. "A taxi. The hospital is just a few blocks away."

Her mouth is tight, but she nods. The security guard is motioning to her from a gate that leads down to the arena.

"Look, Rem." She points to the jumbotron where the replay of my pitiful, but maybe gallant attempt to save Bryce plays on the screen.

I look desperate as I try to hang on, and it's not a good look. Turning away, I get a couple pats—mind the shoulder, friends—as I head back up the steps. As if I'm some sort of hero.

But when I get to the top, I realize something, and a chill creeps through me.

I'm. Still. Here. Still in pain and still watching the catastrophe play out on the screen.

But, *still here*, people. Not back in my time, reuniting with my beautiful wife, or whatever world fate has chosen for me.

Which means—and I'm sure you've already realized it—

Bryce is not my shooter.

I just caused the death of the wrong man.

CHAPTER 14

She wanted to trust him, she really did.

Eve sat on a stool in the lab room, staring at the pictures from the crime scene she'd spent the last two hours developing. Pictures of Leo Fitzgerald's body, pictures of the disarray of the house, and a picture of the telephone number on a Post-It note on the fridge.

Rem's number.

She knew it because she'd called it, more than a few times. And, right now she wanted to pick up her phone and dial it, again.

He'd been there, she knew it in her soul. And he might not have killed Fitzgerald outright, but something he did…

She took a breath and reached for her coffee.

I'm going there to arrest him. His words thrummed inside her. But she knew how things sometimes went south in an investigation.

Still, she'd searched the system.

No arrest warrant.

She took another sip of coffee.

Problem was, she'd heard the rumors about Rembrandt. Knew that some people thought he enacted a little private justice on the side.

For the first time, she believed there was more than a little truth to the rumors.

She needed food. Getting up, she walked down the hall to the vending machine and stared at the meager offerings. Decided on a Snickers bar and headed back to the crime lab.

Silas stood over the pictures at her table. He'd picked up one of Fitzgerald's body, staring at it. When she reached him, he looked over at her. "Rembrandt Stone's handiwork?"

She took the picture out of his hand. "Not necessarily."

"Eve." He stuck his hands in his pockets. "Please."

"We're still reconstructing the scene, but it's possible Fitzgerald fell on his knife, the one he was holding, during a fight."

Silas cocked his head. "This is the same guy your pal Stone went after a few months ago."

"He had his reasons."

Silas raised a brow. "And now you're defending him?"

"First, we don't know it was him." She moved past Silas and set the picture down on top of the one with the Post-It-note. Turned her back to hide it. "Second, Fitz is good for two murders, possibly three."

"And that gives Inspector Stone the right to go vigilante on this guy?"

"He was there to arrest him. Something must have gone south."

Silas's mouth opened. "You knew he was going there?" He leaned in. "Eve. You could be an accessory to a crime, here."

She swallowed, took a breath. "Silas. Just…listen. We don't know what happened. I haven't been able to get a hold of Rembrandt yet—"

"It won't be hard." He walked over to a television hanging on the wall and picked up the remote. Turned it on and flipped to a local news channel. "Wait for it."

She walked over to him, her arms folded. "What happened?"

A few seconds later a newscaster came on, recapping the events of today's Monster Truck Rally. A cold thread wove through Eve as she spotted Rembrandt diving over the edge of the stands to catch a man who'd fallen into the ring. He held him as the man struggled, and she clearly saw a flash of wrenching pain on his face.

The victim fell. She turned away as he hit the dirt, seeing the rest in her mind.

Silas turned it off. "The victim was pronounced dead at the scene."

"Clearly Rembrandt was trying to help him."

"Sure, he was. Apparently, the man was running from the law."

"Silas, I know you don't like him—"

"He's bad for you, Eve. And the thought of you running off to Florida with him—"

"Stop." She rounded on Silas. "I'm not running off. I'm taking a job, one that might change everything for me. And Rembrandt has offered to go with me. Who does that?"

Silas stared at her, something hollow, almost raw on his face. "I would."

"What?"

For a second it looked like Silas was going to leave. He turned, blew out a long breath, then turned back. He ran a hand behind his neck, then, "I love you, Eve. I always have. And…" He met her eyes. "Let me go to Florida with you. Not Rembrandt Stone. We can start over. You and me. Like it should have been."

She'd stilled, her heart in her throat. Took a breath. Then another.

He must have read it as a good kind of hesitation, something in the affirmative because he took a step toward her.

As if what—he was going to kiss her? She held up her hand. "Silas—no—"

He stopped and she hated the hurt in his eyes.

She swallowed, shook her head. "Silas, I—"

"I get it." He took a step away.

"No, you don't." But she made no move to follow him. "You're my dearest friend. But—"

"I'm not dark and mysterious."

"You're—"

"Safe." He met her eyes.

And that shut her down. Because, yes, Silas was expected. He was methodical.

He was safe.

And Rembrandt was out of bounds, off the hook and…dangerous.

And yes, she loved him.

"Silas, I'm sorry. Yes. Rembrandt is dark and mysterious. But he's also sweet and sincere and…you just don't know him."

He held up a hand. "I don't need to. I know what I see." He sighed. "Are you sure, Eve?"

She could almost feel the Post-It-note burning a hole in her pocket. But, she nodded. Probably. Yes.

A tiny, rueful smile drifted up one side of his mouth. "I'm really going to miss you."

His words settled into her bones. "Me too, Silas."

Her cell phone rang on the table and she reached for it. "Shelby," she said, then answered.

"Rembrandt doesn't want me to call you, but I am anyway. He's hurt. Dislocated his shoulder. He got a ride to the Hennepin County Medical Center ER."

"Thanks, Shelbs."

She hung up. Turned and looked again at the pictures. At the body of the man who'd killed her best friend.

Then she picked up the picture of the Post-It-note, ripped it into pieces and dumped it into her trash bin.

She headed downstairs and out to the parking lot.

The sky was clear, blue, edged with the finest wisping of clouds as she drove over to the hospital.

Shelby had probably been working overtime on the thug who'd gotten away—the same thug who'd worked Rem over with a torque wrench. Eve's guess was that she'd tracked the guy down at the rally, and roped Rembrandt into helping her arrest him.

So, if he was helping Shelby arrest the guy from the liquor store shooting, when did he have time to go to Leo's house? Because her father had arrived home from last night's murder scene— the one Rem had been called to—just before she got the call for the crime scene in Montrose.

So, maybe she was overreacting. Maybe he hadn't been there.

Maybe his phone number on the victim's fridge had been a coincidence.

She just needed to ask him. And if he lied to her, then she'd know, right? *I know what I see.* Silas's dark sigh rattled through her.

She knew what she saw as well. The true Rem. But still, her chest thickened as she pulled into the lot.

She flashed her credentials at the nurses' desk and asked for Inspector Stone. They unlocked the doors to the ER and she headed into the back.

She heard him before she saw him, telling someone he didn't need any morphine, thank you. It quirked a smile up her face, but she hid it as she found his curtained station.

He sat on the table, shirt off, the terrible bruising of his shoulder now brutal as his arm hung loose, the bone detached from his shoulder. An ice pack was wrapped around his shoulder but his face bore the pain of the injury, his jaw tight as a nurse fed an IV into the other arm.

"Let them give you drugs, Rem," she said softly.

His expression when he looked up at her contained so much relief, so much hunger, it rocked her back. "Eve."

"Hey, tough guy. Some pretty intense acrobatics at today's monster truck show."

He sighed. The nurse shoved a shot into his vein and he looked at her. "What'd you give me?"

"Just something to take the edge off. It's going to hurt to reset that shoulder."

His mouth made a grim line, but he nodded.

"Something against pain medication?" Eve asked as she came over to take the nurse's place. It unnerved her, just a little, to see him this roughed up. His head wound had turned black around the cut, the bruise dark and ugly. She didn't know why, but she'd always seen him as a little invincible.

"It messes with my head," he said and leaned back on the pillow, closed his eyes. "I'm not sure why I'm even here."

She took his hand. Ran her thumb over the top. "Because you don't stop until you get the job done."

He made a sound of agreement. She took a breath. "Like, Leo Fitzgerald."

His eyes opened. He met hers, his chest rising and falling.

"Rem, were you at Leo's house today? Did you..." she swallowed. "Did you kill him?"

Her heart thumped, the original Post-It-note like a boulder in her jeans pocket. Please.

"I don't know."

Her throat tightened. Oh, Rem—she'd so wanted him to tell her the truth—

He softened his voice. "But, maybe. He had the knife, and I was holding his arm, and we fell, and his throat got slashed. So, maybe."

His mouth tightened. "He claimed he was innocent, and here's the weird thing ... for a bit there, I wondered—and then he said something that told me differently, and I knew...if I didn't stop him, more people would die."

She nodded. "But it was an accident."

"I didn't intend to kill him. That's the truth, Eve."

She knew it, but still, she blinked hard against the burn in her eyes. "What did he say, Rem?"

His jaw tightened. "He said someday he was going to kill someone I love."

His eyes were in hers, hard. And she knew, deep in her gut. "Me. He was going to kill me."

He nodded.

"And, you had a premonition that he was right."

His mouth tightened, but he nodded.

"Thank you for not lying to me, Rem." She offered him a thin smile.

He smiled back, something sweet and delicious and she stepped up to him, leaned past his IV stand and kissed him. Something simple, but his eyes closed as if savoring her touch.

"Sorry to interrupt."

The voice broke her away and she turned to see a familiar face. Tall, blond man, fit, wearing a HCMC fleece jacket and a pair of jeans. It took her a second, then, "Mr. Latsky?"

"Eve, right?" he said and walked into the cubicle. "Bets Mulligan's daughter?"

She stepped back from Rem, still holding his hand. "Yes."

"That's right. How's your mother doing? Still doing her stretches? Her exercises? That kind of wound can tear up the stomach muscles."

"I think so."

He walked up to Rembrandt who let go of her hand to extend his to Latsky. "Gene," he said.

The physical therapist took it, shook it. "I heard you were in here, Rembrandt. Thought I'd stop by and see what kind of work we have cut out for us." He put his hands on Rem's shoulder, moving them gently over his dislocation. "This is an anterior dislocation. Should be able to ease it back into place. I can do it for you, or we can wait for the orthopedist."

"Just get it over with," Rembrandt said.

Gene nodded, his face grim. "Yep." He lowered the gurney so Rembrandt lay flat. Then he took his hand, kept his arm at his side and began to move it up and down, oscillating it slowly, gently, abducting it.

"So, I hear you nearly did a header at a monster truck rally trying to run down a suspect," Gene said.

"Not one of my brightest moves." Rem made a sound deep in his chest.

"Did that that bruising happen today?" Gene kept moving the arm, slowly pulling it away from Rem's body.

"No. Yesterday. Got belted with a torque wrench when I tackled a guy. Same guy."

"You gotta learn how to tackle better," Gene said, grinning. He was adding a bit of traction as he kept oscillating the arm. "I played defensive end in high school, and my coach taught us to tackle mid-body, so they couldn't hit us."

Rem's jaw tightened. "Who'd you play for?"

"Just a small school out of the cities."

Eve's gaze fell on his hand. "It must have been a good team—is that a championship ring?"

Gene glanced at the ring, then at Eve. "Yeah. Went to state our junior year. This hurt too much? I can give you some meds."

"I'm fine." He drew in a breath as Gene reached ninety degrees, rotating his arm externally. "Latsky—I had a buddy who knew a Nick Latsky. Any relation?"

He kept moving his arm up. "This should drop into place soon. Let me know."

Rem glanced at Eve. She had hold of his hand and he smiled at her.

"Nick Latsky was Leo Fitzgerald's stepfather." He looked at Gene. "Name ring a bell?"

Eve frowned at him. Leo had a stepfather named Latsky? She hadn't read that on any of his military records. Gene made a face. "No. I think my mother had a relative named Nick, but…doesn't sound familiar."

Rembrandt gasped, let out a breath. "It's in."

"There you go." Gene crossed Rem's arm over his chest. "I'll tell the nurse to get you a sling. You keep ice on it, and take it easy there, Inspector. It'll heal in no time."

He moved the table back to a sitting position.

"Thanks, Gene," Rem said.

"Glad to help. Let's get you in for a follow up in a week or so, okay?" He turned to Eve. "Say hi to your mother for me."

"I will."

Gene left and Rem watched him walk away. Then he turned to Eve speaking just above a whisper. "He's lying about Fitzgerald."

"What?"

"Yeah. He knows him. He was there, at the bar the day

Fitzgerald and I threw down."

"How do you know?"

He made a face. "Long story. Are you going back to the office?"

"I was headed home, but I can swing back, if you need me to."

"Can you do a search for me?"

"A search of what?"

"I'd like you to track down a guy named Gio Rossi. See if he died in Desert Storm. He would have been a member of the First Infantry Division."

"The Big Red One. The same division as Fitzgerald?"

"They served together. But more than that, they were half brothers." He looked out into the hallway. "I don't know why, but I have a gut feeling we just met a ghost."

With his words, a troubled expression washed his face.

"What's wrong?"

"I just…it's something Fitzgerald kept saying. That he was innocent. That Johnny killed his ex-girlfriends. Even Julia."

"What made you think Fitzgerald did it?"

"The make of the car that ran her down might have been an Olds Toronado. And Fitzgerald's stepfather owned one. His name was Nick Latsky."

Huh. "And this Rossi guy?"

"I'm not sure yet. But Gio is Italian for Johnny, right?"

"Mmmhmm."

"And the name Gene is another version."

"So?"

"I don't know, but something about Latsky feels…I mean, it's a weird coincidence, right? That last name?"

"It's a common last name. Polish, I think. I'm sure we could find two hundred Latskys in the Saint Paul phone book."

He made a face, nodded. "You're probably right." He sighed.

"It's a moot point, anyway. Fitzgerald is dead." He tightened his hand in hers. "I probably need to talk to Booker. Tell him what happened."

"Yes. And while you're at it, you should give him the news."

"What news?"

She slid onto the bed and pressed her hand to his cheek. "That you're moving to Florida to become a surfer."

His eyes widened. "I am?"

"Yes, Inspector, you are." She laughed.

He wove his hand around the back of her neck. "Is that a yes, then, to my question?" His eyes shone.

"You knew I was going to say yes, just admit it."

He smiled. "Yeah, Eve, I did. Deep down I definitely did."

He kissed her. And maybe she also had his gift of premonition, because she knew it, too. In fact, she had a feeling in the quiet parts of her soul that they just might live happily ever after.

CHAPTER 15

Something has gone wrong. And the answer is simple.

Like I said, we chased down the wrong guy. Sure, Bryce was involved, but he wasn't the shooter. He didn't deserve to die.

Someone has to own that.

Agreed, he isn't exactly innocent, but his death keeps replaying in my head, and it's not a pretty place to be.

I would have preferred to have gone back to my apartment, climbed into bed, maybe stared at the ceiling, too scared to move lest I screw up the future.

Better would be me returning with Eve to her place, but deep inside me there's a fear that the longer I stay and the more I'm with her, the more I could wreck my tomorrows and return to a new version of my living nightmares.

I have a good thing going at the moment. And I'm okay with going to Florida. Why wouldn't I be?

I'm open to any future fate has for me, as long as Eve is in it.

But I'm not at my house, and I'm not at Eve's house. I'm standing on the doorstep of Bryce Mattson's house. He lives in a small bungalow in St. Louis Park, and when I say he, I actually mean his parents. Shelby did some math on him while waiting for confirmation of his death, and discovered that Bryce, age twenty-six, lives at home with his mother, his father, and seventeen-year-old sister.

She also discovered I was still in the hospital, found me and apprised me of her intent to inform the Mattsons of Bryce's fate.

I would like to keep my involvement in his death quiet. I could have, and probably should have, ducked out, but the problem is, as you know, Bryce is not the shooter from Jin's Liquor Store. The perp is someone else, and the case is still open.

I mention this to Shelby on the way over to the Metrodome in her cruiser. (My Jeep is still there in the parking lot.)

"What do you mean we got the wrong guy?" she says.

I can't really explain this, can I? Because, as we've discussed, the answer is, "I'm still here." If we'd found justice, the watch, or cosmos, or my own psyche—whatever would have zapped me back to my time.

But that answer would only raise more questions and prompt her to run me back to the ER. So, instead, I say, "I know there was another person in the car. I saw someone in the driver's seat."

"It's not a hunch?"

I look at her, shake my head. "Nope. I'm sure."

She has the decency to pause, and nod. "Well, Rem, I believe you. But the problem is our leads are cold. Bryce died without any clues to his accomplice."

And that's also why I'm on the doorstep of Bryce's mother's home. So I can dig around for more leads.

Because I want to go home.

I don't know what happens if I don't solve this crime. Do I stay here? Do I leave? Booker's words from long ago are in my head. *Don't change the past. You don't know what else you could change, and you could totally screw something up.*

160

He's right. How well I know it. One small change can blow up my entire life twenty years from now.

The doorbell rings deeps in the house and the door opens to a woman in her early fifties, with short graying hair. She wears a sweatshirt and a pair of jeans. She frowns and peeks around the halfway open door.

Shelby identifies herself, and me, and asks if we can come in.

"Of course," Mrs. Mattson wears the look of someone bracing themselves for bad news.

I ask if anyone else is in the house—her husband, maybe her daughter.

She shakes her head. "My husband is at the neighbor's, watching television, and my daughter is with friends."

Shelby looks at me and then turns back to Mrs. Mattson. "We need to talk to about a recent incident."

"All right." She pauses and swallows. "Call me Kerri," she says as she leads us into a family room. It's a small room with a leather sofa that's seen better days, a couple threadbare armchairs. Family pictures line the wall behind the sofa. I stand and look at them as Shelby sits down in one of the chairs.

"Ma'am," she says quietly. "I'm so sorry, but there's been an accident."

Kerri has her arms folded around herself. "Is it Bryce?"

Shelby nods.

There's a moment after news like this is delivered, a heartbeat where the news hasn't hit and disbelief provides a cushion.

In that moment, I sit down next to her.

"Ma'am," I say. "As my partner just told you, it was an accident."

"What was an accident?" She looks over at me, frowns. "What do you mean?"

Shelby pipes up. "Bryce was at the monster truck rally and we—I—went to arrest him on suspicion of burglary." Her voice is even. Solemn. She's doing a good job. "He fled, resisted arrest, and then jumped over the edge of the arena into the monster truck pit." She glances at me and has conveniently left out my role in this event. Maybe I don't want to say anything, either. She'll find out soon enough, but I'd like to be long gone at that point.

My arm is still in a sling under my jacket, I'm bruised, and again I wouldn't be here except for the fact that we need new leads.

"I'm so sorry, ma'am, but he fell in front of one of the monster trucks," Shelby finishes.

Kerri's mouth opens and a trembling hand covers it.

She looks at me, and back to Shelby. "Oh," she says quietly. "I see."

"I'm afraid he died at the scene."

Another beat. Kerri swallows. Her voice shakes. "He was just getting his life back together. He'd come out of treatment. Had a job. He was doing so well." Her eyes are filling, and I wish we'd waited until her family was here.

"He was in treatment?" I ask.

She nods.

"Did he make any friends there?"

She frowns, shakes her head. "I don't know. He went with his cousin, Jimmy, so, he already had a friend."

"His cousin Jimmy?" Shelby asks.

"He got out a few weeks after Bryce. But he got a job, too. I don't know where."

"Do you have a picture of Jimmy and Bryce?" I ask.

She looks at me, nods. Gets up and walks into the kitchen. Her hands are shaking and I feel bad for her. She shouldn't be alone.

"What did he do?" she asks as she rifles through a basket of pictures on the kitchen counter.

"He might have robbed a liquor store," I say, glancing at Shelby.

Mrs. Mattson's mouth turns into a grim line. She pulls out a picture and hands it to me. It's of two boys, Bryce is a few years younger. He's sitting in a picnic chair, his arm around another boy. They might be in high school, although the other boy, who's taller, with reddish brown hair, has a tattoo ringing his neck. A rope, maybe. He's giving a thumbs up to the camera, and the pair is grinning.

The cousin looks familiar, but the nudge is so far back in my head, I can't break it free.

"When was this taken?" I ask.

"Oh, maybe three summers ago, at our cabin."

She's trying so hard to hold herself together. "I don't want to blame Jimmy, but I think he got Bryce into drugs."

My heart goes out to her.

Behind us, the door closes, and I hear footsteps.

"Kerri?" A male voice says. "There's a cop car outside. Who's here?"

She walks past me, takes a breath. "Darrel. Oh Darrel." And now she begins to sob.

Darrel is a big man. Well over six feet. He wears his hat on backwards, has a bit of a beard, and smells, just faintly, of beer. He's holding his wife and looking over her head at us, frowning.

Shelby steps up to him. "I'm so sorry sir, we've come with some bad news."

He inhales a long breath and looks at her, his eyes dark. "I know." He says. "I know what happened."

Then he pushes Kerri away. "Our boy was chased down by a

couple of cops and fell over the edge and they didn't save them."

"That's not true," Shelby said. "Inspector Stone grabbed him. Tried to haul him up. Dislocated his shoulder trying to save him."

I want to reach out and clamp my hand over her mouth because Darrell is in no mood to listen to our explanations. I can see it in his eyes, his demeanor. I grab Shelby by the arm. "We should leave."

He's advanced into the room. "You. You're the one who pushed him over the edge?"

I have one good arm, but he's bigger than me and I don't want Shelby getting hurt. And, more importantly, my Glock is still locked in my Jeep. So, I keep my voice low and even. "I'm so sorry for your loss sir. I did my best, but I couldn't save him.. If you have questions, we'll be glad to answer them down at the station."

He takes another step toward me, pushing past Shelby, and I back up. "Sir. Really. You need to keep your distance."

I'm slowly reaching into my jacket and unhooking my sling from my neck. I'm going to need both hands.

"That was your best?" His voice is more like a growl now than speech. "He's just a kid, and yes, he got into trouble, but you chased him down and you pushed him over the edge—"

"I did not push your son—"

"Shut up!"

I see the fist coming out of my periphery and I can't believe this man is taking a swing at me. But he's drunk, and I have that advantage so his fist lands smack into a cupboard instead of my face. Off balance, he lands hard on the floor.

Then, to my shock, Shelby lands on him. She slaps handcuffs on one wrist, puts her knee in his back and puts his hand in a submission hold. "Stay down!"

Then she cuffs his other wrist.

Behind her, Kerri is screaming, and crying and this didn't go down at all like I might have hoped.

"Mister," Shelby says. "We understand you're hurting. And that you're grieving. And that you're upset. But you don't get to take a swing at my partner."

She hauls Darrell up. He gets to his feet, but he's shaky, and mad and swears at her. Tries to take another swing, but he's wearing cuffs—good thing—and Shelby turns him around. "Okay, let's talk about this downtown."

Kerri steps aside, and I have to admit, Shelby has my respect. Yes, Booker, I think she's ready, and maybe I need to go tell him that before I take off because I'm not sure young Rem will remember the finer points of this encounter.

I don't even realize I'm still holding the picture of Bryce and Jimmy until I'm in the car, and Darrel is sitting behind us, snarling.

"I'll drop you off at the stadium. Can you drive your Jeep with your sling?"

"Yes."

So we swing by on the way downtown and I retrieve my Jeep. But before she takes off, I lean in. "Great job, Shelby," I say. "You're going to make an excellent detective. Maybe even chief, someday."

She laughs. "Right. As if. I think the meds are kicking in. Go home, Rem." She pulls away.

I feel like I've done well this time. My job is nearly finished.

I have a hunch, a real hunch, so I get in my Jeep and head down to HCMC. I turn on the radio and Boston comes on with "Peace of Mind." I turn up the volume, singing along—yes, I'm in that mood, I *need* that mood—and pull into a now familiar spot in the ER parking lot. I should have my name on the space.

I go inside and show my badge. And of course, they recognize me—I've only just left—and I ask for Min-Jin, the owner of Jin's

Liquor store. They give me his room number.

He's on the third floor and I find the nurse's station and ask about my witness.

They point me down the hall. I head down, knock on the door and ease myself in.

A Korean woman in her late thirties sits in a chair reading a book. Next to her, crouched on the floor, is a little girl. Jin-Sun. She kneels on the floor, her coloring book on the seat of a chair, coloring. When she hears me come in, she turns around, and her eyes brighten and she smiles. "Detective!"

She gets up and runs toward me. I hide the grunt as she hugs me, my arm around her, and I'm strangely happy to see her.

"Did you come to see Appa?"

I nod and get up, hold out my hand and introduce myself to her mother.

"Eun-Jin," she says.

If I remember correctly, these two were estranged, but trauma creates second chances sometimes, right? It looks like she's camped out here.

Min-Jin is in the bed, under oxygen. His eyes are closed, and he's sleeping.

"Has he woken?" I ask.

"Just once. He opened his eyes, only briefly, and went back to sleep." She presses her hand to his arm. "But they say he'll recover."

She looks at me. "Thank you, detective."

"You're welcome, ma'am. I was just in the right place at the right time." And you know that's true, even if I did have a head start.

I pull out the picture of Bryce and his cousin Jimmy. "I have a question, and I don't know if you can help me or not. I've wondered if maybe the robbery was an inside job. Maybe one of his employees. Do you know if he had any disgruntled workers?"

She shakes her head. "But we haven't been talking very much lately. We've been living apart."

She looks down as she says it, as if ashamed.

"I understand," I say gently.

She takes the picture, however, and looks at it. Maybe to try and help. But she shakes her head and hands it back. But not before Jin-Sun grabs the picture from her.

"Let me see."

"Honey," Eun-Jin starts, but Jin-Sun interrupts her.

"That's the guy," she says. She looks up at me. "That's the guy who yelled at Appa."

I squat next to her. She's pointing to Jimmy. "This guy here," I ask.

"Yes," she says. "He came in last weekend, and was mad at Appa. I was in the office, and he shouted. He was scary."

"Thank you, Jin-Sun." I'll need to pull the employee records from Min-Jin's store, but my guess is we can cross reference Jimmy and somehow I'll place him at the scene, give him a motive, and even place him in the car with Bryce.

Now I just have to find him.

I'm about to get up when she puts a hand on my arm. "Will you find this bad man who hurt my Appa?"

"I will," I say.

Eun-Jin walks me to the door. Pauses. "Thank you. And not just for my husband, but for my daughter, too. She says she prayed and that you showed up. And that God brought you. I believe he did."

I give her a smile but it's hard for me to believe that God would orchestrate any of this. Then again, my thoughts go back to what I asked my father about God playing games with our lives.

And his answer. *Everything we do is part of that journey to the man you'll be.*

Maybe this is about becoming the man I'm supposed to be. Because I've changed, haven't I?

Maybe.

I sort of like the man who isn't stuck behind the desk, searching for words. Maybe I'm even becoming a man who believes in happy endings. And if that's the game God's playing, I'm in.

I go out to the Jeep, sit there for a moment, and I call Shelby. Her phone goes to voice mail. "I think I found who we're looking for. Call me when you get this."

I hang up. It's then I see that Eve's called me. She hasn't left a message, so I call her back.

No answer.

Maybe she found the whereabouts of Johnny. She said she was headed home, so my guess is that's where she's going to be. Admittedly, I also want to see her, maybe submit to some TLC, so I drive over to Uptown, then to her cute house in Webster Avenue.

The front walk is cleared, but her car isn't in the driveway.

I pull up. Look at the house.

Maybe she's still at work. I entertain a small fantasy of building a fire, making her dinner, starting the version of the life I know, and miss.

She's so easy to read—I find her key in a lock box behind the drainpipe, and let myself in. The house is quiet. I take off my shoes, my jacket and go into the kitchen.

It's full of memories—recent ones—of kissing her, here in this kitchen. And the night we spent making soup, then camped out by the fire.

We're going to have a good life. The perfect life. Here, or Florida or Zimbabwe.

Because she loves me.

I open the pantry, and see that she's still eating boxed dinners. Not a vegetable in sight in the fridge, either.

So maybe we'll get takeout.

I manage to wrestle some logs into the kitchen from the deck Sams built last summer, and it's not long before I have a fire going, something warm and friendly.

I start to relax—the drugs are kicking in—and I look at my watch. It's still early, although night has descended. I call her again.

Voice mail. Which means, I hope, that she's on her way home.

I sit on the sofa, and my body reminds me I'm hurt, so I agree to lay down.

Close my eyes.

We're in the backyard, staring at the sky as Eve sits on my lap, in my arms. Ashley is playing on her swing set, and I realize it's a memory. That last beautiful moment before my life imploded.

I've made a decision. I pull out my cell phone and dial up Booker. He answers on the second ring. "Rem?"

"Before you say anything, I need to tell you that I don't want it."

"What? Where are you?"

"Eve's house." I sit up, and notice the fire has died to embers. I must have fallen asleep. "Listen. I don't want the watch."

Silence. "Rem—"

"Seriously, Booker. When I get back, if I still have it, I'm destroying it. Throwing it into the lake. Driving over it with my car—something. So, don't even it give it to me. I'm going to live with things the way they are."

"Before you—"

"I'm tired of trying to fix things. And before you say anything, I can't just leave it alone. I can't watch people suffer. I know you

169

went back and found Mickey's killer, but…we still lost him. I know how that feels, John, to lose someone, and justice isn't enough. I have to stop it…which means I can't help but change time."

I've walked to the window, and I see headlights pull up into the drive. Eve, finally, home.

"Rembrandt, we need to talk."

"No. I don't know how long I have here. And…" Oh no. I glance at the clock.

It's nearly forty-eight hours. And Shelby hasn't called me back. And…as I look out the door, I see a figure—a man—not Eve, getting out of the car.

"Booker, I gotta go—" I head to the front door.

"Wait—"

But I hang up, because I have to call Shelby. But before I do, I open the door.

Everything stills as John Booker stands in the glow of the porch light.

"Chief."

His jaw is tight. Then he closes his eyes, as if pained. "I've been looking all over for you, Rem."

I look at my phone. Four missed calls. I don't understand…

He climbs up onto the porch and something in his eyes—call it a hunch, call it a reflex, even call it *time* laughing at me—makes me reach out for the jam.

"What?"

But I'm too late. Because I can hear it—the rush of wind, and this time, a shrill beeping, as if I've run out of time. The world tilts, and I fall forward.

Booker catches me, but I hit my knees.

"Are you okay?"

I put a hand down on the cold, snowy porch, and look up at

him.

"I'm sorry, Rem—"

Then he's gone, because I'm snatched up, caught up in the vortex of time.

And my world goes black.

CHAPTER 16

Usually, according to the rules and my experience so far—I return to my present day a minute into the future, in the same place I left.

When I left last time, I was sitting in the cab of Danny Mulligan's truck outside Groveland Cemetery, the rain pattering on the windshield. Mud saturated my suit—I'd left shortly after Eve's burial to track down the watch Booker gave me. The watch I thought still might be on his body, now encased in cement in the graveyard. Desperation drove me to the unthinkable, you can guess what I did.

Frankie, Booker's daughter, and Zeke, another cop, found me at the bottom of his grave, my shovel pinging against the coffin.

Frankie had the watch I was looking for, found in the belongings Booker left behind.

I took the watch, got into the truck, wound the dial, grabbed the file and prayed. No, *hoped.*

I can hear the pattering of rain as time brings me back, as my vision clears. I'm still sitting in the truck and I'm still cold, but oddly sweaty as I push myself up from a prone position on the seat.

I'm not at the graveyard. A wan streetlight shines on a brick building, and a quick survey suggests I'm parked in a skinny alleyway lot.

It looks a lot like Quincy's gym downtown, where Burke and I work out the knots of our job with a semi-daily boxing match. It's just for exercise, and maybe a little therapy and I take it as a good sign that I'm not parked at the graveyard, again.

But of course I'm not. Because, as you know, Leo Fitzgerald is dead. And Eve is then, alive.

And maybe, even, Ashley. *Please, God.*

And here I am, praying again.

Music pumps out of a door on the side of the building—Ozzie—and a light over the top of the door illuminates the faded sign and confirms my hunch. *Quincy's Boxing Gym.*

I don't know why I'm here, but my head hurts, like it did in the past, and I touch my eye and find it tender. Like I've recently been in a fight.

In fact, my entire body is sore. I flick on the dome light and glance in the mirror.

Yes, my eye bears a recent run in with a fist, but my face is leaner, my hair cropped short, and I wear a shadow of a beard. I notice the faded white scar from the torque wrench parting my hairline near my temple and run my fingers over it.

It's then that Booker's words return to me. *I'm sorry, Rem.*

Sorry for what?

A banging at my window jerks me, and I turn.

For a moment, I don't recognize the man staring in at me, his face only inches from the window. He's young—early thirties, maybe, and wears his hair buzzed at the sides, with a mop on top, his jaw tight, his eyes hard, and he's wearing a black tee-shirt soaked to his skin.

And then, recognition kicks in. Zeke Kincaid, my protege.

He's dating Frankie Booker.

And, right now, he looks like he wants to strangle me. I open the door. "Zeke, what's up?"

His eyes widen. Then he shakes his head. "Okay, whatever. Vita is looking for you, and if you don't go in there and finish this, we're in big trouble."

You know the question—finish what? But that's how it is when I re-enter my life.

I have to catch up, and quickly. It's a little like swimming upstream, into a waterfall. "Right," I say, and get out.

He steps back and looks me over as I shut the door. "Vita said you might bail after the last fight, and I see why. Maybe you're not up to this."

I frown at him. Maybe not, but I don't want to suggest it. Zeke, too, looks a little worse for wear in the dim light—his jaw bears a bruise, and his left eye is bloodshot.

"Listen," he says, coming close. "You have a rep, which is good. This guy is already afraid of you, and that works to your advantage. But, he also has something to prove, so…don't let him."

Shouts from the gym erupt through the door, and Zeke glances toward it, back to me. "Sounds like it's over in there." He takes a breath. "You're up, Ivan."

I raise a brow.

"The Terrible, get it?" He grins at me.

Not really, but I nod, and he grabs the door just as another man bangs through, out into the dark drizzle.

He's middle-aged, but lean, medium height, blond and carries a Russian vibe. Especially when he grins, showing a couple gold teeth, and says, "It's time, Staz."

I look at Zeke, but clearly the man is talking to me, so I turn back to him. "Right."

"He's ready, Vita," Zeke says, and slaps me on the shoulder, then shoots me a last look and holds open the door.

I follow Vita in towards my fate.

Quincy's has been overhauled since my last visit, two days ago. Plywood covers the windows, and the boxing rings have been removed, replaced with squares taped on the floor. Around it, men shout, the redolence of sweat, blood and vodka in the air.

I've entered Fight Club.

I glance at Zeke, frowning. He gestures to Vita, who has parted the crowd for me, to lead me into the center of the ring.

Oh boy.

Standing in the middle is a younger man—late twenties, tops. He's big, well over 6'6, maybe 225, and thickly muscled. His shirt is off, and he's a real piece of work. I spot a couple scars on his torso—knife wounds is my guess. And a scar trails down the side of his face, from his eye to his jaw.

He has dark eyes, and my guess is that he works as muscle for some local mobster. The fingerless gloves he's strapping on are barely padded, and now I know why I hurt.

Vita steps to the middle. "You all know the rule. If you want to run one of Alexander's crews, you must match Staz in the ring—three rounds, and you must be standing at the end. Meelis Lazo here thinks he has what it takes."

I look over at Meelis and I don't think I want to be in ring for three rounds with the kid. For one, I'm not as big. Second, I don't think this is my first fight of the night.

Third, I'm not sure who Alexander is, and why I work for him.

Vita turns to me, smiles. "Knock him out, boss."

Boss?

I reach to take off my watch, and with a start, realize it's gone.

Maybe Booker took me at my word and kept the watch.

I take off my shirt, because I can move better, and the crowd creates a perimeter around us as I glance at Zeke. I must wear something of dread on my face because he gives me a grim look and nods.

I walk over to him, lean in and hand him my shirt. "What is going on?"

"Listen, this guy has chops. He's fought in a few off-book fights and has a perfect KO record. I'm not sure how he's parlayed this into a tryout for Malakov's team, but he's here, and you can't afford to let him win. He's on Boris' leash, and if you let him in, we have a mole. You have to knock him out."

The only word that makes sense in all of that is Malakov—a name I remember from my last reality. Alexander Malakov is the head of a Russian gang that recently declared war on the Minneapolis Police Department, my beautiful Porsche 911 a casualty of said war.

And now I work for him? Worse…

I'm his hired thug?

No, this can't be right.

I turn around and get a glimpse of myself in one of the big mirrors that still grace the walls of Quincy's. In the speakers overhead, Fleetwood Mac plays "Dreams," and I'm not sure I'm not heavily medicated, because I'm ripped. I almost don't recognize myself, honestly, because I've put on nearly twenty pounds of muscle, all of it upper body.

Maybe I *can* take this guy. Except, let's remember I'm old. I might have bulk, but I'm not sure I have stamina.

And everything just hurts more when you're fifty.

I'll have to be quick, get him down fast, and be willing to take a few hits to land the power punches, mostly because, as I size up this guy, my guess is that he has nearly a ten-inch reach advantage.

This is going to hurt.

He'll use his jab—it's the best one to inflict pain. And I'll have to catch it, dodge it and land a counter jab of my own.

I'm oddly jazzed, suddenly, for the fight, and I'm not sure why. Maybe it's the cockiness of my opponent, grinning at me like I'm an old man. It ignites a fire in my belly.

But, more likely is the fact that the sooner I get this over, the sooner I find Eve, right?

Suddenly Zeke shouts at me to level the kid, and I surrender to the sweat and noise of the crowded room. Let's do this.

From the opening bell—or shout from Vita, really—Meelis comes at me. I occupy the center lane, steady on my feet, guarding my face and occasionally move my head off the center line. He doesn't draw blood.

I do. He's desperate and presses in, throws a right hook. I see it, pull back and counter with my own hook.

His head snaps back, and his nose is bloodied.

That has to hurt, but he just blinks the pain away and nods, fury in his eyes.

I'm not mad. I'm not desperate. But I am determined.

I want to go home.

He jabs at me, and I keep blocking them, moving closer. He throws his weigh into the next punch, I sidestep it and slam my fist into his ear.

He goes down on a knee.

Cheering. Apparently I have fans.

Meelis shakes his head, as if clearing it, and staggers to his feet. I glance at Zeke and he's standing at the edge of the crowd, his arms folded, nodding.

Listen, I'm not trying to make a point. I'm just trying to

survive.

Meelis swings hard and lands a blow on my shoulder but I step in and put two fists into his gut.

He staggers back, the wind stripped from him. A couple of his cronies catch him, let him find his breath.

I dance back, turn to Zeke. Raise an eyebrow.

Zeke nods, something solemn in his face, then shouts and I turn just as Meelis connects with a right hook.

Pain explodes through my entire body, I spin and nearly go down, scrubbing my hands on the floor.

He hasn't broken my nose, but it's bleeding and I'm seeing splotches.

Okay, I'm done. So ready to walk away from whatever little game we are playing here.

Zeke walks over and helps me up, grabs me by the arms. "Staz. Get it together."

"That was a cheap shot," I say, wiping my nose. But Zeke just nods, so I turn, and now I'm mad.

I might be smaller than this guy, but I've spent twenty years learning these moves. I dive in, ready to end this. He broadcasts every punch, and I see it before they land. I ride them, move with them, adapting to Meelis' speed and rhythm.

He's breathing hard, still bleeding, and it's time I break him. I back up, as if he's got me, hoping he'll chase me.

He does, and throws a telegraphed right hand. But he's too far away, the punch is a wide miss and I deliver the prize—a left hook, right hand combo.

He counters, of course, but I duck. And offer a perfect upper-cut that Meelis never sees. Two steps backwards, and he's down.

And with his hands covering his face, it's pretty apparent he's not getting up.

I might have broken my hand through the glove, but as I stand over him, breathing hard, I know it's finished.

I return to Zeke who hands me a rag for my nose and a bottle of water. I'm breathing hard, and spill some water over me, and then turn.

"Anyone else?" I ask.

Vita grins at me. "Oorah!" he shouts to the crowd. Meelis has crawled back to his cronies, and I feel a little sorry for him.

He's young and angry and I might need to watch my back.

The crowd disperses—I see a few dollars change hands—and Vita comes over to me. "Alexander wants to see you."

Are you kidding? I have somewhere to be. "Now?"

"Now," he says, and I grab up my shirt and follow him toward the gym office on the second floor. We climb the stairs—the walkway overlooks the workout pit—and move along the edge to one of the glass doors.

Although I've never met him, I know Alexander Malakov. He runs the Brotherhood, the Minneapolis version of the Bratva, and has ever since Burke and I took down Hassan Abdilhali, a Somali warlord who ran the city twenty years ago.

He's lean and strong, dark haired, is wearing black pants and a black dress shirt, and is smoking a cigarette, standing in the walkway as we approach.

"Good fight, Staz," he says. I nod. He gestures inside his office and I follow Vita and Zeke in.

Alexander closes the door, walks over to his desk and pulls out a bottle of vodka, sets it down. Then he adds four shot glasses and fills them, quietly.

He sets one in front of me, hands Vita and Zeke each one, and lifts his own.

"To Staz, still unbeaten."

I raise an eyebrow, glance at Zeke, but he's grinning, not looking at me, and he shoots down the liquid.

Fine. It burns, but settles in my gut.

"So, will you let him work for you?" Alexander asks.

I'm assuming he means Meelis and I take a moment to consider that. Then I lift a shoulder, as if I've thought this completely through. "Maybe. Or maybe I'll just kill him."

He laughs. What have I gotten myself into?

Where am I? And please don't tell me I actually *work* for Alexander Malakov.

Alexander thumps a hand on my shoulder, then leans down. "Don't forget about our little problem with Mayor Vega."

Mayor Vega. Finally, a name I recognize. I want to breathe out in relief, but instead I nod. "I'm on it."

He gives my shoulder a squeeze. Leans up. "Good job tonight. It's good for the boys to remember who is in charge."

I think he means me.

He opens the door, and I take it as my cue to leave. Zeke is behind me, although Vita stays.

I bee-line to my truck.

Zeke says nothing until we're standing next to it. Then I round on him. "What was that?"

He looks at me, nonplussed. "What was *what*?"

"The fight. The meeting with Malakov—all of it. What is going on?"

He looks past me, then behind him. "Staz, I don't know what you're talking about. You okay?"

I stare at him. His words, his confusion sound *real*.

More, "Where's Burke."

He frowns, shakes his head. "Burke who?"

I open my mouth, close it. "I'm going home."

A fist has formed in my gut as I get in the truck. I leave Zeke standing in the alleyway, under the drizzle.

The city is unchanged. I drive through downtown, get on Hennepin, take it to Lake Street, then past the lake to Drew Avenue.

As I pull closer to my house, I note that the big elm is gone. Funny, but maybe time has reset and I chopped it down recently. And, through the dim light of the streetlight in the alley, I spot a swing set.

I want to weep, my heart big in my chest. I pull up the drive and park outside—Danny's truck doesn't have the remote garage door opener—and climb the steps.

The door is locked. Of course it is—I always tell Eve to keep it locked. But it means I have to knock.

It's late, and I don't hear footsteps, which is strange because usually Eve waits up for me, but...

But maybe I'm undercover, right? That feels right. I'm undercover, working to take down a Russian mobster.

Although, is Zeke undercover too? Has to be, right?

No one answers and I finally lean on the bell. I hate waking her, but I don't have keys.

Footsteps sound on the stairs, the familiar creak of the third riser sounds, and I'm already smiling.

The door opens.

I recognize the man standing there, although it takes a second. He's tall, wiry and has the red hair of his mother, Bets. "Asher?"

He's bare chested, wears a pair of pajama pants, and he's staring at me with a stripped look. "Rembrandt?"

I nod, frowning. "What are you—do you live here?"

He stares at me like I'm drunk. "Of course I live here," he says. He hasn't invited me in. "What are you...how..."

He takes a breath, looks past me, and then opens the door. "You'd better get in here before someone sees you."

What?

But I step inside and he shuts the door. Presses his hand to his mouth. Shakes his head, his gaze on me, like he's seeing the ghost of Jacob Marley.

"What?"

I look up the stairs. Maybe he's still my roommate. I want to run upstairs, burst into my bedroom, wake up my wife, but his words stop me. "Did anyone see you?"

I frown at him. "What? No."

He breathes a sign of relief. "Okay, then."

"Asher, you're sort of freaking me out—"

"What are you doing back here, Rem?" he says now, pulling me into my office. It looks different—my desk has been replaced by a chest of toys, a bookcase, a pop-up play tent. And my heart does a double take. Ashley is here.

"You shouldn't be here."

His words are a slap. "Why not?" Please, let us not be estranged, or worse, divorced.

"Whadda you mean why not?" He frowns at me. "Because you're a murderer."

CHAPTER 17

He's right. I am. You know it, I know it.

I murdered Leo Fitzgerald. Even if I didn't put my hands on him, you were there, you saw it.

I'm guilty of his death.

Although, I am surprised that Asher knows this. I stare at him, all words gone.

"Daddy?"

The voice is soft, light and sweet and rushes through me, taking my breath.

Ashley?

Asher puts a finger to his lips. "Stay here."

What? No. I turn even as he leaves the room and am about to come out of the shadows when I see a little girl descend down the stairs.

She has reddish blond hair, wears a Frozen nightgown and has Eve's face.

But it's not Ashley. Asher gets down on one knee and puts his arms around her. Picks her up. "What are you doing out of bed, Evie Bear?"

I can't move. *What?*

He looks back at me, shakes his head, then climbs the stairs.

I can taste my heart.

Something suddenly feels very, very wrong.

I'm standing in the kitchen, looking out the window at the swing set, the moonlight glazing the yard when Asher comes back down.

I turn to him, swallow. And we stand there, looking at each other a long time before, "You can't stay, Rembrandt. I'm sorry, bro, but…it's too dangerous."

Dangerous.

I breathe out. "Fine. Just…tell me where Eve is."

I've put together a small scenario in his absence.

Somehow, I was made for Leo's murder. I get that—I wasn't the most sly of murderers. And maybe Eve couldn't stand the heat and moved to Florida. I get that too.

I might have even served time. It would account for my body bulk. And maybe, when I got out, I needed a job. Like working protection for a Russian gangster? Doesn't sound like me, but I've had a few variations of my past, and this isn't terribly far-fetched.

Maybe Zeke, my protege, came with me.

Maybe my name really is Staz now.

I put my hand on a chair, because the whole thing is just preposterous.

But that's okay. I'm tired of trying to change the past, trying to get it right.

I just need Eve.

We'll start over from here.

Asher is looking at me, his eyes glistening, and he shakes his head. "Rem. Seriously. You have to stop doing this to yourself."

What?

Oh. She's married to someone else. Fine. Okay, I've lived through that version, too. I'll survive.

"Who? Burke?"

He frowns. "Burke?—what? Are you crazy?"

"Who is she married to?" And if he says Silas, I might just… well, there's no way that's happened.

He looks away, an expression of cutting pain on his face. "Seriously? Have you been drinking?"

Not the way he's thinking, but yes.

"Should I call someone? The chief, maybe?"

Shelby?

"No…I just need to know where Eve is. Then I'll be out of your hair."

He pushes out a long, low breath, then walks over to the counter. Picks up his cell phone.

"Hey," he says, his voice low. "You'll never believe who showed up at my door." A pause, then. "Huh. Yep. I don't know what to—okay. Yes."

He hangs up and sighs, then walks over. "Stay here. The chief is on the way."

"Just tell me where she is, Asher."

He closes his mouth. Swallows. "Where she's been for the past twenty years, Rem."

Florida.

"The Groveland Cemetery."

I open my mouth, and now my stupid knees decide to buckle and I slide to the floor.

"Rem!" Asher comes over, crouches next to me.

I can't breathe, my words caught in my tightening throat.

"You're freaking me out, Rembrandt."

"No." My breathing is ragged and shallow. I stare at him, and

187

my words barely emerge. "How did she die?"

Asher shakes his head. "You can't go through this again. It cost us too much. Just…you have to let it go—"

"How did she die?" My voice is fine now, raised.

"She was murdered! Sheesh, how much have you had to drink?"

"Not enough." I get to my feet. "Who murdered her?"

Asher has backed away. That's fine. I'm scared of me, too. "Maybe you should go."

"Who murdered her?" This time my voice is low, lethal.

He holds up his hands, and I see one of Eve's looks, when she's exasperated, flash through his eyes, although his holds a little fear, too. "No one knows."

What?

"It's a *cold case*, Rembrandt. Come on! What is wrong with you!"

I stare at him. "Everything." Then I push past him, and head for the door.

Except—*wait*. I stop, my hand on the knob and turn. "Who did I murder?"

He's shaking his head. "You need medical help."

"I need more than that. Just for fun—who did I murder?"

His mouth tightens. "Andrew Burke."

Of course it's Burke.

I stagger outside, down the steps, over to my truck. I get in and sit there as Asher comes to the porch and stands in the outline of the door, his arms folded.

I don't know where I'm going, when I pull out, into the rain-slickened night, but I end up at my maybe pre-ordained destination all the same. I park right where I started, turn off the lights and stare at the chain link fence.

Then I get out. The gate is closed, but I vault it easily and stalk up the hill.

Unfortunately, I know exactly where I'm going.

I find the stone right where I left it, only now it's aged, the white marble filthy from the rain.

Of course, there's no small white marker next to it.

I sink down in front of it and press my hand to the lettering.

Eve Mulligan, beloved daughter.

The date is my yesterday, and with a jolt, I hear again Booker's words. *"I'm sorry, Rem."*

No. No. No! I'm on all fours, because it feels like the only correct position to begin to beg. Appropriately, I press my forehead to the grass, clutching it.

And I weep.

It's brutal to hear your own screams, the rending of your soul. Even in the padding of the rain, and night, I'm shaken through, and I'm unashamed of my grief.

It is finished.

Because you know the rules. I *must* return to a cold case, and I have no new cold cases before Eve's.

Even if I do use hers, I arrive *after* her death.

And let's not forget…I don't have the watch. Because I told Booker I'd throw it into the lake.

I'm an idiot.

Eve is dead, and I can't change it.

The wrenching weakens me, and I find myself curled against the stone, my hands over my head.

I don't hear the car door, the footsteps, even the breath of the man until he crouches in front of me and puts his hand on my shoulder. "Rembrandt," the voice says softly.

I still. And look up. I have nothing as I stare up at him,

breathing hard,

Chief John Booker has come back from the grave to rescue me.

He meets my eyes, the old lawman suddenly revealing a hint of compassion.

"What did I do?" I say to him.

His mouth tightens into a grim line. "More than you can imagine." Then he holds out his hand. "I've been waiting for this moment for twenty years. C'mon, rookie. Buck up. This isn't over yet."

Rembrandt Stone's epic series concludes in two months. Check out a sneak peek of book six. Join us in November for the final installment.

THE TRUE LIES OF REMBRANDT STONE

BLOOD FROM A STONE

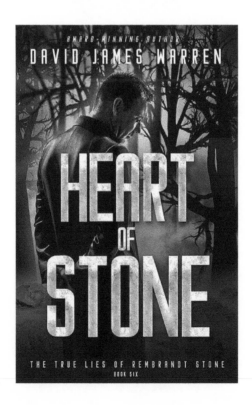

HEART OF STONE
CHAPTER 1 - SNEAK PEAK

They say that without hope, people perish.

I say hope crushes the soul.

That's why I look away when Frankie Booker's hazel-green eyes fall on me as I walk into Sergei Malakov's third-story office.

The pulse of some electro-dance beat pumps in from the nightclub below, the odor of bodies and a hint of reefer saucing the air. Turbo is on fire tonight, the line to get into the club a half-block long despite the sultry July-heated night.

Sergei leans against the front of his desk, his arms folded over his gray silk Brioni dress shirt, his cuffs rolled up—as if he'd actually do any of the bare knuckles work it takes to keep his multi-million dollar organized crime empire running.

That's why Vita called me. Sergei's "XO," the guy who delivers his orders. Vita is shorter than me, lean, blonde and about my age, his face heavy with lines and a scar that runs from his eye to his chin.

We're work friends.

"Staz," he says in greeting and I nod at him and walk over to

Sergei. The female—she can't be Frankie, not right now—sits on the sofa. I can't tell if she's been roughed up, but I don't look at her, just in case.

"Thanks for coming," Sergei says from his perch on the desk.

"Of course, boss." I've played the undercover game for years, so this can't be any different. Booker briefed me earlier—wait for that, I'll catch you up—and apparently, I've been at this game for years, so sliding into my persona as Staz, Malakov's right hand thug is an old shoe.

According to my sketchy research, Sergei Malakov runs the biggest Russian gang in Minneapolis, filling the void after Burke and I took down Somali warlord Hassan Abdilhali some twenty years ago. According to Booker, Malakov's also recently declared war on the police department, hoping to carve out his own little Moscow in the North Loop.

I remember this part from past versions of my life—my 1994 911 Porsche having recently been a victim of this war.

And I know you're wondering—past versions?

Again, wait for it. It's worth it, I promise.

Sergei is vaping, and now sets down his cigarette. My guess is that it's filled with high end snow because he's edgy and ticking with energy. I walk over and put a hand on his shoulder. "You okay?"

"How did she get in here?" He directs the question to Vita, and I look at him, expecting an answer, too.

"I don't know. She had the code to the door. She won't say where she got it," Vita says.

Now I look at Frankie.

The sight of her makes me pinch the corners of my mouth and take a breath. Her lip is bleeding, although that could be from a struggle. Frankie has it in her to cause trouble, thanks to her parentage.

I know for a fact that Booker doesn't know what she's up to. But then again, she's in her mid-twenties and can make her own decisions.

If she were my daughter, I'd put a tracker on her.

Okay, not really, but the thought catches me, and I inhale sharply.

I had a daughter. Once upon a happier time. With blonde hair and blue eyes and the kind of laughter that made me believe in things like hope, and faith, and love.

For the last month, I've tried to believe—to hope—that I could find her, save her, bring her home. I haven't succeeded.

Remember what I said about hope?

Sergei brings me back to point when he says, "Staz, I want you to find out where she got the code." He looks at Frankie. "Make her tell us." He then looks back at me. "And then get rid of her."

Frankie makes a sound, just a small one, from the sofa, and I wonder if it's for show. But when I look at her, and she lifts her gaze to me, a real tear drips down her cheek.

I wonder if she knows me, this smart, vibrant, nosy daughter of my mentor.

Probably not. Because according to her father, I've been playing this undercover game for many, many years.

To the world, I am Staz Kalenin, head of security for the Sergei Malakov, head of the Brotherhood in Minneapolis.

My head still pounds where I took a hit last night in a fight down at Quincy's—and it wasn't a spar—where two bros go a couple rounds in the ring—but a real fight, with thin gloves and blood and the sound of breaking bones.

I won, but it hurt.

"Maybe she got lost," I say to Sergei, about Frankie. I gesture to her with a head bob. "She doesn't look like trouble."

Okay, she does. She's dressed in a leather bustier, a pair of black shorts and five inch heels. Booker's head would explode if he saw her.

And I wonder, suddenly, where Zeke is. When I last left them, in our previous lifetime, Frankie and he were dating.

Ah. The light shines upon my pounding, webbed brain. Zeke had the code to Sergei's office.

I have no doubt Frankie lifted it from him, somehow.

"She's trouble, all right," Vita says and walks over to her. I think I save both Frankie and my life when I don't move as Vita grabs her dark hair and yanks her head back. He leans over her. "Maybe, after you talk to her, you give her back to me."

I know the Brotherhood traffics women, and I'm not sure he doesn't mean to sell her.

Yeah, that isn't happening. But I lift a shoulder. "We'll see."

Her gaze darts to me and for the first time I narrow my eyes at her, something that says, *I got this.*

She glares at me, so maybe she didn't quite pick that up. Then she plants her heel in Vita's ankle.

He shouts and I cross the room and grab his wrist as he reels back to slap her. "Get out," I say.

Vita is in charge of operations, so technically, I don't answer to him.

I think.

Vita jerks away and looks at Sergei. He too has gotten up, picking up his e-cigarette. He nods to Vita, who informs me of his current emotional state with a word, then they both leave the room.

The door closes, and suddenly we're alone.

I have a gut feeling Vita is standing right outside the door.

She looks up at me, and tears course down her cheeks. But her eyes are bright, as she says, "I know you won't hurt me."

Really? Because remember what I said about hope? And you saw Vita…

One of us is probably going to die.

MEET
DAVID JAMES WARREN

Susan May Warren is the USA Today bestselling, Christy and RITA award–winning author of more than eighty novels whose compelling plots and unforgettable characters have won acclaim with readers and reviewers alike. The mother of four grown children, and married to her real-life hero for over 30 years, she loves travelling and telling stories about life, adventure and faith.

For exciting updates on her new releases, previous books, and more, visit her website at www.susanmaywarren.com.

James L. Rubart is 28 years old, but lives trapped inside an older man's body. He's the best-selling, Christy Hall of Fame author of ten novels and loves to send readers on mind-bending journeys they'll remember months after they finish one of his stories. He's dad to the two most outstanding sons on the planet and lives with his amazing wife on a small lake in eastern Washington.

More at www.jameslrubart.com

David Curtis Warren is making his literary debut in these novels, and he's never been more excited. He looks forward to creating more riveting stories with Susie and Jim, as well as on his own. He's grateful for his co-writers, family, and faith, buoying him during the pandemic of 2020-21, and this writing and publishing process.